Keith Salmon initially studied pharmacy, before training as a creative flavourist with Unilver.

He has since become a chief executive in the City of London, worked in litigation support on both sides of the Atlantic, and as a freelance consultant to many Government departments.

Keith currently lives in the Scottish Borders with his wife.

Immigration!

www.olympiapublishers.com

OLYMPIA PAPERBACK EDITION
Copyright © Keith Salmon 2014

A CIP catalogue record for this title is
available from the British Library.

ISBN: 978-1-84897-424-1

(Olympia Publishers is part of Ashwell Publishing Ltd)

This is a work of fiction.
Names, characters, places and incidents originate from the writer's
imagination. Any resemblance to actual persons, living or dead, is purely
coincidental.

First Published in 2014

Olympia Publishers

60 Cannon Street
London
EC4N 6NP

Printed in Great Britain

I dedicate this book to all the hardworking, intelligent members of the Civil Service who tried to do a good job while being obstructed by their political masters.

Acknowledgement

To the many people in the various agencies and services who spent so much time explaining to me what they do and what they would like to do.

Immigration!

James Greene stretched out behind his large desk on the sixth floor of Lunar House, Wellesley Road, Croydon, South London. As the new Home Office Minister he was the Head of Immigration for the UK Border Agency and this was his first day at work. He also had an office at 2 Marsham Street, London, but he preferred Croydon.

"If you make a success of this posting, who knows what will be offered," they said and James was determined to succeed; in fact, "failure is not an option," he repeated to himself with undiminished enthusiasm. To him, immigration was everything at that moment. He could not understand those who had warned him against accepting the promotion. *Jealousy,* he thought, *that's all it is: nothing more.*

He was young, only thirty-two in fact, with his sights set firmly on promotion as quickly as possible, leading to one of the great offices of state and who knows maybe, among his equals, to become the first. However, that was just a cliché for James who did not acknowledge any equal. It was war; dog eat dog and he would have done anything to secure more political power. Long ago he had learnt to keep his opinions to himself, to listen intently to those in power, to time his actions and to act decisively, relying on his own judgement. On the two occasions he had got it wrong, he was able to say that he had been misled or had innocently misunderstood his instructions.

Because he was seen to be the obedient slave of those in power and because the people he blamed were invariably those perceived as threats to the powers that be, he managed to absolve himself of his political sins, mortal though they were.

And there he sat, looking down the length of Wellesley Road, the main road in Croydon and across into the Whitgift Centre, basking in his power and dreaming of things to come. He was woken from his reverie by a knock on the door. "Come," he said and in came a smartly dressed middle-aged man holding a thin manila file in his right hand.

"Good morning Minister," he said, "I am Sir Robert Pennington, the Permanent Under Secretary for the UK Borders Agency. Welcome." James said nothing but looked imperiously at the senior civil servant. It was a look that had served him well on many occasions and more than anything else, certainly not a brain, had contributed to his reputation as a hard man. There was a long silence.

"Well?" he asked.

"Well, Minister, I am here to welcome you to the Agency and to inform you that if you need to know anything, I am here to help." Sir Robert sat down on a comfortable red leather chair opposite his political master.

"So what do I call you? Robert or Permanent Secretary?" asked James Greene.

"Sir Robert will be sufficient, Minister," was the reply.

There was another icy silence after which James said, "Well then, I'll call you when I need you. Good day."

The Permanent Secretary counted slowly to five, then rose and turning at the door said, "Good morning, Minister."

"It's a tough job," they had told him when he had accepted the promotion. "You've got a juggling act on your hands. Up to now, every Immigration Minister has failed and disappeared

14

into a political wilderness. So don't underestimate the task."
Despite listening attentively and nodding gravely to the advice
given, James had such confidence in his ability that he refused
to acknowledge any challenge. He merely replied, "What kind
of challenges do you think I might face?"

"Four major tasks, I think," said David Lingham, his
Parliamentary Private Secretary. He continued, "The first is
this infernal view held by the Agency that it is for us to prove
that an asylum applicant has no right to reside in our country.
Anywhere else, it is the applicant who has to convince the
relevant authority that he or she has the right to stay. You've
got to get that changed as a priority. Secondly, when we
process asylum seekers or catch illegal immigrants who then
claim asylum, we refuse to lock them up and, as a result, they
disappear into the black economy. It's your job to get these
spongers banged up to rights while we process their bogus
asylum claims. Your third task is to get the foreign national
criminals, who plague our green and pleasant land, out of here
and back to their tin-pot little African hovels. Your fourth task
is to get the lazy staff in the Directorates of your Agency off
their arses and get us a decent 'Tipping' result. Lastly, you have
to achieve all this at no extra cost to this Government." He
paused.

"No problem," said James quickly and confidently. "It will
be done."

"I hope so, James," said David. "All eyes will be on you.
Good luck." James left the meeting room.

He walked down Victoria Street to a plaza opposite Victoria
Station where he entered a very fine tapas bar. He ordered a
particularly good bottle of Ribera del Duero and two glasses.
He was shown to a table for two in the window.

"Tosser!" A voice boomed from the doorway. James looked up, smiled and stood up. They shook hands eagerly and shook hands again.

"Wanker! How are you?" asked James.

"Bloody good; better for seeing you," answered William Dean, a forty something Divisional Director of ABN AMRO a leading bank in the City of London. "How's it going, then?"

"Total max out," James replied. "I got it! I got the top job! Just now!"

"What? You got Immigration? You jammy bastard! What do I call you now, Minister or Right Honourable Wanker?"

"Minister will be sufficient, you bloody tosser," and he laughed loudly. "It's bloody good to see you again. I'm glad you could come to lunch."

"How could I refuse people in high places? Never know when I might need you to pull me out of a bit of creative insider trading and, if you ever need a mortgage, you know where to come."

"I can always get a mortgage from my bank," replied James.

"Not the kind of deals I can arrange; ones where you don't pay anything, except my very healthy commission." They both laughed and emptied their glasses.

Little did either know that at the same time Sir Robert Pennington was speaking with John Prendergast, a Deputy Secretary at the Home Office. It was a telephone call that would have far reaching effects for James Greene.

"How's the new boy?" asked John.

"As obnoxious as they come. It will be difficult to work with this one," was the reply.

"Then I suggest we bring him to heel," said John. He continued, "Let's try the phased strategy that we usually use in this situation."

16

"Oh, you mean the 'Forty-nine Steps' don't you?" replied Sir Robert.

"Indeed I do. The most effective Ministerial training course we ever invented."

Sir Robert remembered this particular training course, one offered only to very senior members of the civil service and then in total secrecy. You might be led into believing that the course has forty-nine steps to it but you would be wrong. The title of the training course relates to the means by which Mr Memory (in the John Buchan book) was able to store vast amounts of highly technical information in the back of his mind and then release it by means of a secret word instilled under hypnosis. The two key aspects of this secret civil service technique were, firstly, an intensive training course in which everything the Minister said would be remembered verbatim and forever and, secondly, the transmission of an auto-suggestion key whereby any aspects of these memories could be recalled instantly.

There are other highly secret aspects of the training course and I am not going to tell you what they are. For God's sake! If I told you they wouldn't be secret, would they? Anyway I don't consider that you have a right to know these things.

OK, I will tell you one. It is this:

As each Ministerial statement, that is, speech, command, order, insult, tantrum, etc., is stored away in the memory, another aspect of the training course comes into action. In the storing away of the new memory, the sum total of the memories stored to date is summoned and a risk assessment is automatically performed by the mind on that entirety. The resulting risks, which are categorised as red, yellow and green, depending on their seriousness (red being the most immediate and damaging), enable the senior civil servant to avert the

Minister from the risk situation. Alternatively, it is also possible to steer the political master directly into an unforeseen hazard. Now you may say, 'surely the Minister would foresee the most obvious risk, like being ambushed by the press or misleading the House!' You would be right. That is why one would seldom use a category red risk to damage a Minister, unless he was particularly stupid and unpopular. No, it is the medium risk category which is so useful in this context.

And this is what was decided that day, on the telephone.

"Right, Robert, you can rely on me to bowl your man a couple of yorkers every month," said John Pennington.

"Thanks John. How's your boss?" asked Robert.

"Sir Joseph Malthouse?" was the reply. He continued, "He's doing well. Odds on him becoming the next Cabinet Secretary when Sir Norman retires."

"So, you'll be the next Permanent Secretary to the Home Office then?"

John sighed and said, "One only lives to serve one's country, Robert."

Sir Robert replaced the phone and pondered the events of the conversation. "I'll call you when I need you", was what the little pompous shit had said. *OK*, thought Sir Robert, *I'll leave it to you to find out what is happening. Don't expect me to tell you.* And with that he left the office, intent on having lunch with his Grade Two Director, Kenny MacDonald.

Immigration is Complex

"Why the fuck didn't you tell me about this?" stormed James Greene at his Permanent Secretary, who was standing in front of the particularly fine George III mahogany desk.

"Yes, I will sit down, Minister," replied Sir Robert. "To what are you referring?"

"This! This!" shouted Greene, throwing the newspaper across the table at Sir Robert who picked it up (no, not the table) and read the front page headlines.

'New Minister plans to throw immigrant women and children into prison!'

"I see," said Sir Robert. He continued, "What is your problem, Minister?"

"Are you a total imbecile? Have you got no fucking brain in your head? This is absolute nonsense!" Greene replied.

"Minister, are you saying that this newspaper article is inaccurate in some way?" Sir Robert perched ready for the kill.

"Of course it's fucking wrong! I never authorised this!" said Greene, almost purple in the face.

Sir Robert opened the manila file in front of him, read from it for fifteen seconds and said, "But you did, Minister. I have here your expressed view that you no longer wanted asylum seekers to be released into society while the Agency considered their claims. You said, and I quote you, 'It's my job to get these spongers banged up to rights while we process their bogus asylum claims'." He slid the memo across to his political lord and master.

"Who the hell leaked this to the press?" demanded Greene, somewhat subdued by the turn of events.

"Not this Agency, that's for sure. Indications are that it came from the Home Office but we can't be certain. I can't investigate it any further. I'm sorry Minister."

"Why can't you? You're my Permanent Secretary aren't you?" asked Greene.

"Indeed I am Minister but Sir Joseph Malthouse is the Permanent Secretary for the Home Office and I am not going to confront him with a half-baked accusation. I suggest you take it up with the Home Secretary but I would caution you." Sir Robert paused looking at his Minister.

"Caution me!" exploded James Greene. "Caution me, with what?"

"Precipitate action," was the reply. Sir Robert noticed the blank expression staring at him from the opposite side of the desk. He continued, "Minister, this is your second day in your job and you have a major crisis. It's best to slow down a bit; to think and then try to calm down the whole situation. Nobody will blame you for this minor event. It happens all the time to Immigration Ministers and you must remember that …

"Immigration is complex."

Sir Robert observed the effect of his words on James Greene, the Minister for Immigration and thought *that was easy. Jesus, he's such a gullible shit, misleading him is not even pleasurable. I must stack a few things in his favour so that each defeat and his public humiliation will be worth the candle, at least.*

"So, how do I get out of this, then?" asked James timidly after a lengthy pause.

"Let me arrange a meeting with the paper's editor. It's best to have it over lunch because by the main course he'll probably be blind drunk."

"You mean he'll be open to suggestion, maybe see things in a different light?" suggested James Greene.

"He'll be lucky to see things without double vision," replied Sir Robert.

"Then what's the point of the lunch?"

"Minister, he'll be so pissed that the next day, he won't know what he agreed to at lunch. I'll probably slip a small brief to him while he's stonked out of his head!"

James paused for a moment and diffidently said, "I suppose I should thank you, Sir Robert."

"Not at all, Minister," replied the Permanent Secretary. He continued, "It's my job after all, to see to it that you are safe from the media and, if I may say so, from yourself, at times."

He looked across the desk and saw a small, insecure child of a politician, remembered all of the spoilt child's hurtful words and smiled as he left his Minister's office.

Just as Sir Robert had said, lunch was absolutely fantastic, more than that it was amazing, sumptuous, elegant and regally formal. James remembered Sir Robert's words of advice: "It will be very formal, Minister, at least black tie unless you feel that we should make a more direct statement and insist on white tie." James had decided that the most formal expression of the importance of his stately office would be appropriate. Sir Robert observed the result in less kind terms, which could be summed up colloquially as mutton dressed up as lamb.

"I've had a message from *The Guardian*, Minister. Their editor can't make it for lunch but will join us for drinks afterwards," said the Permanent Secretary.

Sir Robert and his Minister dined at the Garrick Club, which is situated at 15 Garrick Street, Covent Garden and devoted to members of the literary profession. Indeed its former members have numbered Charles Dickens, William Makepeace Thackeray, Anthony Trollope, HG Wells, AA Milne, and Kingsley Amis. The Garrick Club was founded at a meeting in the Committee Room of the Theatre Royal, Drury Lane on Wednesday 17th August 1831 but only moved to its newly-built clubhouse in Garrick Street in 1864.

To say that William (call me Bill) Fillingrue-Smythe was fat would be an understatement, akin to the popular misconceptions of an honest politician, a talented modern artist or an unbiased, educated female social worker. Bill was grotesquely obese; weighing in at twenty-eight stone, he was a serious danger to every chair which bore his weight and sustained it as a tribute to its design and fabrication. However, he was the current editor-in-chief of *The Guardian* newspaper, the most left-wing rag, purchased by modernist communists, radicals, vegetarians and social workers. He arrived formally dressed in white tie and covered in a copiously-cut black cashmere overcoat. He extended his hand and said:

"Robert. Lovely to see you again. How are Mary and the kids?" They shook hands and smiled warmly.

Turning towards his Minister, Sir Robert said, "May I introduce the Minister for Immigration, Bill?"

Almost immediately the warmth disappeared from the editor's eyes, which became as cold as ice; his smile however remained fixed and large.

"Minister," he said. "What a pleasure to meet you." He maintained his grasp, which was surprisingly firm, on James Greene's hand.

James said nothing but continued to look imperiously at the fat newspaper man. There was a long silence. It was broken by Bill who said:

"Yes, a real pleasure, Minister." He leaned forward and covering the Minister's right hand with his left, continued, "One of many occasions, we would hope, eh?"

James felt slightly queasy touching this fat, inebriated man who was trying to ingratiate himself. He vowed never to meet him again.

They sat in the main lobby and a steward took their order for drinks. James ordered a bottle of Peroni; Sir Robert chose a pastis, while Bill ordered a triple Glenmorangie with a spot of water. "Brings out the bouquet, you know, Jim," he said, laughing too loudly for the occasion. However, his eyes retained their icy stillness. James winced slightly at the use of the diminutive of his first name.

"Marvellous place," continued the editor. "I really like the nosebag here. I hear it's really good." He looked directly and intently at James who smiled weakly and looked away. "Yes, I always like to get the proverbial in the trough!" boomed Bill. "Sorry I couldn't make it today, damned editorial deadline, I'm afraid." He rubbed his hands together and the drinks arrived. Bill downed his in one go and said, "Thank you, I will have another." James pushed aside his glass and drank from the bottle. Sir Robert added a little water to the pastis which immediately turned white.

"So, what's your problem, Jim?" asked Bill.

James Greene winced and replied, "I wish you would call me James or Minister."

"Of course you would; of course you would," was the riposte as Bill leaned forward and squeezed the Minister's knee. He continued, "So what's your problem?"

Sir Robert stepped in quickly saying, "I think the Minister feels that he has been misquoted; that your paper has misrepresented his views on immigration."

"Is that right? Is that right? I thought we had quoted him verbatim. In fact, I have a copy of the internal Home Office memo from which we wrote the article," said the editor, opening his briefcase and passing over the document to James Greene, who read the signature on the damaging document. It read 'John Prendergast, Deputy Secretary, Home Office'. James had never met him and vowed to learn much more about this combatant.

"Did you not seek to ask the Minister for his views on the subject? After all, he was central to this matter. Do you not think that would have enabled you to write an unbiased article?"

Bill slightly spluttered, downed his whisky and mumbled, "Well, yes, maybe but we've got deadlines to meet you know. It's not like you lot in Government with all the time in the world and no accountability, not like a normal job, mmm?"

"As if the likes of you would know!" exploded James Greene, giving the editor an imperious look.

"Minister, are you saying that my newspaper writes biased articles?" James started to speak but Bill cut him short with, "Or maybe you are saying that its editor is incompetent or perhaps ignorant? That would make another fine article. Listen to the headline, Jim: *'Immigration Minister says that The Guardian newspaper and its editor are ignorant, incompetent and its coverage biased when it wrote: James Greene, the Immigration Minister, said, it's my job to get these spongers banged up to rights while we process their bogus asylum claims'."*

James Greene sat silently glaring at the editor who continued, "Minister, you really must understand that all

Ministers, including you, have a relationship with the press. You can't avoid that but you can decide what direction that relationship might take." He paused and looking intently at the Minister said, "Which direction would you like, Jim?"

The stony silence that resulted was eventually broken by Sir Robert who suggested, "Bill, I am sure the Minister is not looking for a confrontation with your newspaper. It's just that he wishes an article to be fair and unbiased, telling both sides of the story. In fact, I am sure he would agree that the best way to achieve this would be a series of exclusive interviews with you, just to ensure that he is given a fair chance to put the record straight. Don't you agree, Minister?" Sir Robert turned to his Minister, at the same time giving him a forceful kick on the leg.

"Well, yes, so long as it's fair," James replied.

Bill considered the situation for about ten seconds and then said, "I will have another thank you, Minister," holding out his empty glass to the steward who took it away for replenishment. "That would be a most encouraging situation, one in which my newspaper would engage enthusiastically and sympathetically, striving to represent the best interests of our valued government contact." His drink arrived, which he downed in one. He continued, "Thank you, Minister, for a very enjoyable meeting. Lots of good stuff to think about."

He rose and was beginning to turn away when Sir Robert said, "As a sign of good faith, Bill, the Minister thought you might like this briefing paper. I'm afraid it's small fry compared to the last memo but every little helps, doesn't it?"

They all shook hands and Bill left the lobby.

When he'd gone, James said, "What a thoroughly unpleasant man. Do we have to deal with him?"

"Well it's up to you Minister but I would advise to keep him on side. You never know when he could be useful," replied Sir Robert.

The headlines in the next day's Guardian read: '*Immigration Minister calls the Editor-in-Chief ignorant, incompetent and his articles biased. A secret government memo obtained by this newspaper confirms that James Greene also thinks that his staff is, and I quote, "a lazy bunch of overpaid, incompetent people who wouldn't get a job where they had to work for a living." The memo gives details of the two Assistant Directors, working for the Case Review and Support Directorate in Fleet Street, who spend four days each week at home, looking after their children and the fifth day in back-to-back meetings so that no departmental business has been conducted for the last two years. Apparently, this is called the "work-life balance".*'

"I want a copy of that memo," demanded James Greene.

"I thought you might, Minister. I have it here," said Sir Robert, retrieving it from his manila file.

James Greene read the author's name: 'John Prendergast' it said.

Sir Robert smiled inwardly. This was the memo that he had given to Bill at yesterday's liquid lunch. The Minister had agreed his action and there would be plenty more opportunities to make him famous. *I must speak more with John,* he thought, and left the Minister who was deep in thought at that moment.

Immigration Makes
Strange Friends!

"I don't know what I'm doing wrong," said James Greene to his colleague, the Minister of Home Affairs, who sat quietly regarding him.

Liam Burns MP was the bald-headed, forty-five-year-old Member of Parliament for the River Cole Valley, near Birmingham. Being six feet two inches tall he posed an impressive figure of a 'man about the House' and he used this image to promote his political interests of gambling, immigration and road safety. Indeed, he had been in charge of the UK Borders Agency for a considerable time before escaping to the Treasury, where he presided over its technical bankruptcy. As a consummately accomplished government minister, he was knowledgeable, sure-footed, shrewd and politically astute. Seldom putting a foot wrong, he adopted a forcible and vindictive managerial style that unnerved all but the strongest political opponents and kept officials from the junior to most senior firmly in their place. They were there to do his bidding even at times when he, himself, did not quite know what he intended.

He was a herd animal. Those of his political party were, most definitely, his staunch friends; anyone else, including his constituents, were his bitter enemies. He had seen how the fickle electorate could be his adoring supporters one minute only to turn against him treacherously for reasons not even known to them. Although a staunch Roman Catholic, he believed in himself and his ability. However, he was not a Humanist, just an egotist.

"What's your problem, James?" he asked.

"I don't really know. It's just that everything I do seems to go wrong," replied James Greene.

"Be specific; be factual!" said Liam stentoriously.

"Well, it's just that damaging articles keep appearing in the press about my proposed intentions. I've seen the leaked memos. I don't seem to be able to stop them."

"Do they have a name on them?"

"Yes, they do. It's John Prendergast. You know him, don't you?"

Liam paused for a moment and said, "Of course I do. He's one of our Deputy Secretaries here at 2 Marsham Street. Be careful of him, James, he has the ear of Sir Joseph Malthouse, who's next in line to the Cabinet Secretary."

"So I believe. How do I stop these leaks?" asked Greene.

Liam paused further and then said, "You have to ask yourself how Prendergast is getting hold of your secret agenda, which he then shamelessly and overtly turns into memos ready for leaking. He doesn't have this information readily to hand so someone is feeding it to him. Someone high up in your Agency."

"Who? I mean, there's no-one who knows my agenda. That is, no-one but my Permanent Secretary, Sir Robert Pennington, but I'm sure he wouldn't leak. He spends most of the time defending me and repairing the damage caused by these leaks to the papers," replied James Greene.

"You know, matey, you're your own worst enemy at times," said Burns. He continued, "How else would Prendergast get this information? Who else would have timely access to it? You know that Pennington and Prendergast are members of the same fencing club? Yes, they were both senior members of the civil service team. They won a couple of international trophies."

"I didn't know," replied James Greene.

Burns thought deeply and then said, "OK. Got it! Let's play the man and see how he likes it. What's your most sensitive agenda item, James?"

"Oh, that would be our idea to utilise spare prison space throughout the EU to bang up criminals, foreign nationals especially."

"An excellent idea," beamed Liam Burns. "I don't know why I never thought of it." He sat back.

James continued, "Well, it certainly makes sense. We can't keep building prisons in the UK and those we have are in a state of woeful disrepair. I can't understand people's opposition to us banging up our scrotes abroad. They'd probably enjoy much better cells there than we can offer them here. However, there would be none of this Human Rights nonsense, no soft living and studying for law degrees in their spare time. It would be hard labour for the lot of them. You can bet they wouldn't like it at all."

Liam smiled and said to his friend, "And which countries were you thinking of?"

"Anywhere really that has spare capacity and wants to earn a bob or two," replied James.

"You mean, Holland, Denmark or Norway?"

"No, no, not those touchy-carey-feely places. I'm not sending our criminals to a holiday camp. I was thinking more of Romania and Bulgaria where we can rely on the Mafia over there to make sure that none of the inmates escape. I thought of the sort of deal where we pay the prison one dollar per day per prisoner, provided they don't escape, in which case we pay nothing, zero, nada. It's not a bad idea, is it?"

"Right," said Burns and continued. "You'd be letting yourself in for heavy criticism if this leaked out. I mean we all know the Human Rights records of countries like Romania and Bulgaria."

James leaned forward eagerly and said, "I disagree entirely. These are EU member states and we all know that to become part of the European Union, a country must satisfy the most rigorous checks and balances concerning upholding citizens' rights. So, the public can't have any legitimate concerns over prisoners being maltreated or injured."

"Are you seriously telling me that a Romanian prison cell would be a bed of roses for one of our home-grown prisoners?"

"Of course not! It'll be a rude awakening for them but it won't breach their human rights, that's what I'm saying. And as for our nasty foreign national criminals who come to the UK then rob, rape and threaten us while on benefits, they will see a very abrupt change in their lives, that's for sure."

This was the first time that he had seen his friend, James Greene, so animated. He was impressed.

He leaned forward and said, "OK. This is what we do. Firstly, you write a speech about how you feel strongly about safeguarding the human rights of prisoners, especially foreign nationals, in the UK. Pennington will probably ignore it because there's nothing he or Prendergast can use to damage you. Secondly, you get one of your backbench friends to write an article absolutely vilifying foreign national criminals and demanding that they be deported to EU jails; give him your secret agenda so he can bulk it out a bit. Then write a memo to him saying that until you know more about it, you can neither support nor condemn the proposition. Say you might support it if the detail stacked up. Encourage him to say that you are in support of it. Now, at the same time, write to one of your Assistant Secretaries saying how much you deplore racial bigotry, especially when attached to immigration. Date and time your internal communication. OK so far?"

James nodded. He continued:

"Right, now get your backbench colleague to send a copy of the article to your Agency, saying that you support the views contained in the article. You can be sure that Pennington will leak it to Prendergast, who will leak it to the press. Sit back until it's done and then present Pennington with your internal memo to your Assistant Secretary and ask him how he can reconcile the situation. After that, summon Prendergast to an intra-departmental meeting, with Pennington and Sir Joseph Malthouse, express your outrage and threaten to call in the Home Secretary. That should put them on the back foot." Liam Burns sat back smiling smugly.

James Greene, for the first time during the meeting, started to smile and said, "Thanks, Liam. Thanks a lot. That should sort them out."

"Not quite, James," said Liam, "but it will certainly rock their pompous foundations of perceived impregnability. Anyway, it's worth a go just for the laugh of it. Who knows how many will come out in support of you? Immigration makes strange friends you know James."

The next week, *The Guardian* ran a front-page article saying: '*James Greene, our (by now) famous Immigration Minister wants to send all of our petty criminals to an ex-Soviet hard labour camp in Romania. So, if you have been wrongly convicted of stealing a can of baked beans from Tesco, you could find yourself breaking stones for the rest of your life in a foreign jail.*'

James Greene adopted a look of imperiousness, for which he was famed, and said to John Prendergast, "Well?"

"Well what Minister?" was the reply.

James took a deep breath silently and said, "You might well ask what Minister because I am going to have your job for this insolence."

Sir Joseph Malthouse leaned forward slightly and placing his horn-rimmed glasses on the table in front of him said, "I think that might be somewhat excessive, if I may say so Minister." He leaned back convinced that he had managed to turn the tide.

"You may well say so, Sir Joseph, but you would be quite wrong." He turned to John Prendergast, one of the two Deputy Secretaries of the Home Office and continued, "Your man, here, has leaked a completely false document to the press, one which has libelled me and damaged the Government. There's no doubt about it. His name is on the internal memo which was leaked to *The Guardian* and you, John Prendergast, will pay for this insolence."

"We cannot be sure who leaked it, Minister," continued Sir Joseph, somewhat unnerved but managing to keep his composure quite magnificently.

"His name is on the leaked document, therefore he's guilty, if not of leaking it personally, then at least of gross incompetence regarding security. These are secret documents, you know," James stressed.

"But Minister, I thought you said they were false, libellous which by its very definition means untrue," said Sir Joseph Malthouse, sitting back and beaming at an angry Immigration Minister.

"Sir Joseph," said Liam Burns, leaning forward with eyes piercing the Permanent Secretary of the Home Office. "I wonder whether or not you appreciate the seriousness of this situation. In fact, I do detect a certain amount of flippancy in your attitude to what could be a serious threat to this Government's ability to execute a key strategy of its published manifesto." He continued, "This leak from your department," he paused to allow his words to find their mark "must have come from the highest level for who else would have access to the memos of your Deputy Secretary?" Sir Joseph opened his mouth to speak but Liam merely waved away any comment with the back of his hand and continued, "Is this the first leak of information from your department concerning the Minister for Immigration, Sir Joseph?"

Sir Joseph, somewhat apoplectically, exclaimed, "Of course it is! Do you think this department is a sieve?"

Liam Burns MP turned to his government colleague and asked, "Is that true, James?"

"It certainly isn't. Twice before articles have been leaked to the editor of *The Guardian* and twice before they have been signed by John Prendergast here and they have always criticised me in the vilest terms."

"Not in the vilest terms, Minister. It was the newspaper articles that criticised you, not my memos," said John Prendergast, slightly less confident than at the start of the meeting.

"So it would appear to me, Sir Joseph, that you are unaware that your department has a history of leaking high security key aspects of government policy and it would also appear that you are remarkably unperturbed by it," said Liam Burns, sitting back and looking over his hands at Sir Joseph.

Sir Joseph finally said, "I am outraged by your suggestions. Never in my forty-two year civil service career has anyone dared to say such things to me or my staff!"

Liam Burns retorted, "I say it! And I say it again in case you did not hear me! But there is worse for you, Sir Joseph. I have ordered an external departmental enquiry by Special Branch into who persistently leaks this damaging information about HM Government's Immigration Minister. It's someone within your department without a doubt and, when we find out, I will make it my personal crusade to teach you and your department a lesson they shall not forget." He turned to Sir Robert Pennington and said, "I will expect you to co-operate with your Minister in every way. Do I make myself clear, Sir Robert?"

Sir Robert, shocked beyond belief, merely nodded vigorously and mouthed silently the words, "Absolutely, absolutely."

When they had all gone, Liam turned to James and said, "That's how to do it; divide and rule. We've now got Pennington so scared that he won't leak anything else and Prendergast is worried shitless about what the external enquiry will reveal, so he'll keep his nose clean for a long time to come. That only leaves one person."

"Who?" asked James.

"William Fillingrue-Smythe," was the answer. "I suggest you offer him a knighthood, James."

The headlines of *The Guardian* blazed, 'Editor-in-Chief honoured by Her Majesty for a life dedicated to journalism. William (now Sir William) Fillingrue-Smythe has been made a Knight of the Order of the Bath by the Queen in recognition of his efforts for a free and democratic press. It is envisaged that Sir William will be invested at Buckingham Palace in the autumn. *The Guardian* says: "Well done, Bill!"'

"Bill Fillingrue-Smythe, how can I help you?"

"Bill, what the hell have you done?" said James Greene to the editor of *The Guardian*.

"What do you mean?" was the reply.

"I've just read the front page of your newspaper."

"Yep! It's great isn't it?" replied Bill.

"You're not supposed to let it be known until you receive your special letter from the Palace!" said James Greene.

"But it's confirmed, isn't it?" said a nervous Bill.

"Look Bill, there's a protocol here that has to be followed. You just can't assume. It has to be confirmed," said James.

"But there's no problem is there James?"

"Well I don't know how the Palace will view what you've done. You'll just have to wait and see."

"But you said I'd got my K, James. You said it!"

"I know Bill but I didn't say plaster it all over your newspaper. Anyway, just let it be, Bill."

They hung up and James sat back in his large swivel chair and, looking up Wellesley Road in Croydon, thought to himself, *you've got as much chance of getting a K as I have of sticking my head up my arse.* He walked over to his ornate sideboard and, pouring himself a large malt whisky, said, "Yes, I will have another, Bill."

Immigration and the British

"We all know about immigration and the British. There's no need to explain it to us, Sir Donald," said Paul Souveryns, a Deputy Commissioner for community agriculture with the European Union in Brussels.

"How do you mean, Paul?" asked Sir Donald Evans, the British Ambassador to the EU.

"Well, you cannot stand it. Everyone knows that you hate allowing foreigners, even we Belgians, into your precious little country," was the reply.

The Ambassador paused for a moment and then spoke. "Paul, I really do think that you need a lesson in history about this issue." He relaxed into the comfortable armchair, took a sip of his twenty-year-old Armagnac and continued, "Back in 1946, just after the Second World War, it was Britain who said that Europe needed some kind of charter to safeguard citizens' rights against another monster like Adolf Hitler; a charter to maintain a person's automatic right in law to life, freedom from torture, a right to family life and freedom of speech. We asked around our allies and they, being busy repairing their countries from the devastating war and occupation, told Britain that if we felt so strongly, then we should get on and draft something. So, it was left to a senior British civil servant to draft the Treaty of Vienna, a treaty which would form a shield behind which every person fleeing from torture or oppression could hide, confident that we would protect him or her. These high-minded principles were adopted when the European Convention of Human Rights was created and ratified in 1951. So, Paul, without the British there wouldn't be an EU Convention." He paused to let his words sink deeply into the arrogant Deputy Commissioner sitting opposite him.

He continued, "We, in Britain, feel deeply for the plight of others. We are renowned for our desire to come to the aid of the underdog. This is well known and, because of our high-mindedness, people take advantage of us; people like you Belgians and especially the French who have had no love for us for almost a thousand years. You offload your immigration problems onto we British who, most of the time, are too polite to tell you where to get off. Now that's the truth about immigration and the British." He sat back, studying his opponent's face.

"I think this is totally unfair," said a small, balding man dressed impeccably in an Armani suit. He continued, "We French have always been at pains to assist the UK in the control of migrant workers, as you know, Sir Donald."

"Maurice," said Sir Donald, addressing his French counterpart, His Excellency M. Maurice Fournier, the French Ambassador, "you know as well as I that this is nonsense. Your officials at the Sangatte Refugee station in the Pas de Calais exert absolutely no control over the inmates who just flood into the UK from that place. They stow away in lorries, cargo trucks or walk down the tunnel and your guys do nothing to stop it!"

"But this is not true!" exclaimed the French Ambassador. "Just the other week we caught eight illegal immigrant men who were hiding in a British lorry bound for the UK."

"Yes, one of your customs officers threw a tear-gas grenade into the back of the lorry and then bolted the back doors so that the unfortunate sods couldn't escape. They were stuck there, in a terrible state, until the lorry arrived at its depot in Slough two days later," was the reply.

"But it taught them a lesson, ne c'est pas?" Maurice paused for a moment and said, "You British are far too soft on these migrant slimes. They come to your country, do not work, claim your benefits, steal from your people and give venereal disease to your women and, what do you do? You blame the French. We do not allow this scum into our country."

"No, you send it to Britain when, under EU law, *you* should be processing their asylum claims," Sir Donald replied.

"That is not altogether true, Sir Donald. We send a few back to Italy when we wish to have a good laugh. You see, the officials there have problems understanding the immigration forms, in fact, most of them can't read. It is, how we say, très amusant." Maurice sat back and sipped his small black coffee.

"So how is this going to solve our problem?" asked Kenny MacDonald, a diminutive Scotsman sporting a shock of ginger hair. He was a man of considerable presence who, although only five feet four inches tall, was the match for most people he encountered. As a Grade Two director with the UK Borders Agency, or UKBA as it is commonly known, he was one grade below the Chief Executive and a further two grades below the Permanent Secretary. Although there are two grading structures within the Agency, with the Chief Executive being the highest of the executive branch, there is also another career structure leading to a Grade One Permanent Secretary. It's a strange system which seems to function well but how has always set me at a loss.

Kenny MacDonald was born in Maryhill, a very rough area of Glasgow some forty-nine years ago. His parents were very poor: his father worked in one of the shipyards as a carpenter and his mother took in washing. It seemed that Kenny would be destined to follow either his father or maybe his brother, who was a welder, into one of the shipyards. However, it was a scholarship awarded by Strathclyde University that was one of the turning points of his life. He read mathematics and his quick, perceptive and analytical brain made short work of a first-class honours degree. To everyone's delight, he decided to stay on for his Master's degree and was destined for great things, until he received news of the death of his father from a massive heart attack, followed two days later by his mother's suicide.

He joined the Immigration Service, as it was then called, and rose steadily up the ranks mainly due to his many qualities but especially his surefootedness, honesty and academic excellence. He perceived most of his colleagues as lacking a depth of knowledge of their disciplines, manifested in superficiality and insincerity. He tolerated none of this in his many daily meetings and was well known for silencing any fool who attempted to dilute the high quality of his agenda. He was known for speaking his mind and he cared little about the seniority of the recipient. He had been warned many times to tone down his manner but he ignored this, stating that it was his duty to deal with his issues as he saw fit. More senior managers had tried to remove him from office on several occasions but he merely defied them and their attempts failed. His managerial qualities were well known and, if not liked by everyone, were certainly admired. He looked around the table at his colleagues and, once again, saw superficiality replacing scholarship.

"So, how is this going to solve our problem?" he asked.

"I believe it is very simple," replied Paul Souveryns confidently.

"I believe not," was Kenny MacDonald's answer.

"But it is a very simple matter in law and therefore I am confident that it will not be a significant issue for us. The law applies to everyone," said Paul wearily.

"Perhaps someone should then remind you of the seriousness of this problem. David, please explain to this meeting the nature of the problem we are facing," said Kenny.

David Lawson, a nervous thirty-two-year-old Assistant Secretary from the Special Cases Directorate cleared his throat and started to speak. "Our problem concerns Andrej Rakic, who was a Serbian warlord until last year. He commanded about two thousand of the most vicious of the Serbian troops; they even named themselves 'The Panthers'. Their loyalty to Rakic was absolute and their mission was to rid Serbia of all Muslims." David sat back.

"How many Muslims did they kill?" asked Kenny.

"About eighty thousand men all in all," was the reply.

"And how many women were killed?"

"About the same number."

"Tell us David, how were the women killed?" asked the Director.

"It was quite gruesome, Mr MacDonald. Most of the women were lined up and the men who wanted to rape a particular one formed a line in front of her. Then they took her one at a time, usually in front of her husband and children. Sometimes there would be twenty men on one woman." David stuttered for a moment, clearly overcome with grief. He continued, "Then they slit her throat in front of her husband after her children had been killed."

Kenny MacDonald looked around the table at the faces, which had suddenly lost their expressions of smugness, only to be replaced by increasing horror. He continued, "David, I know that this must be very distressing for you but I must ask you a few more questions." David nodded and Kenny asked, "Please tell us about the children. How many children were slaughtered by Rakic's soldiers?"

David said, "About one hundred and twenty thousand is our best estimate but it might have been far more; it's difficult to get reliable statistics under the circumstances."

"About one hundred and twenty thousand," repeated Kenny and then continued, "And how did they die, David?"

David Lawson was clearly distressed but, after a minute or so, said quietly, "When Rakic's troops entered a village, they normally rounded up all the people and after they had separated the men from the women, they built large bonfires and then threw the children, many of them babies, onto the pyres. Usually this was done in front of their mothers." David broke down into tears, unable to suppress his emotions any longer.

"Eighty thousand men killed. Eighty thousand women raped and slaughtered. One hundred and twenty thousand children and babies burned alive, watched by their mothers," said Kenny MacDonald. He continued, "And you want to give asylum to this butcher, Rakic?"

"He has a right," said Paul Souveryns. "There has been a regime change in Serbia and if he stays there, he feels that he will be tortured and killed."

"I can think of nothing better for him," Kenny MacDonald said quickly.

"But he fears for his life!" exclaimed Souveryns. "He has the right to a life free from torture and death. These are his rights under the European Convention of Human Rights."

"And what about the rights of his victims?" boomed MacDonald. "They were human as well, in case you have forgotten!"

"Yes, that was a most unfortunate event but we must not let it cloud our judgement," said Paul.

"So, we are going to let him land at Terminal Two, Heathrow Airport and just calmly grant him indefinite leave to remain in the United Kingdom, is that it?"

"Yes," replied Sir Donald. He continued, "But I would be interested to hear what you would suggest we do with Rakic."

Kenny MacDonald took a deep breath and said quietly, "Allow him to land at Heathrow, take him into custody, march him round to the back of the building and put two bullets in his head. That's the way to deal with this problem properly." He sat back glaring at them.

Paul Souveryns jumped to his feet shouting, "But this is barbaric! It is against all common decency! It is against the law! You cannot do this! You just cannot!"

Kenny MacDonald was deep in thought by this time and merely thought, *I wonder. I wonder.*

Immigration Makes
Many Enemies!

"He's a shit! He's an absolute, bloody shit!" said Bill Fillingrue-Smythe to John Prendergast, sitting opposite him in Axminsters Restaurant in Mayfair.

Axminsters is a truly amazing place for anyone who loves fine British dining. It has been serving the finest British food since 1742. The menu includes wild fish, shellfish, game (when it's in season) and meat dishes sourced from the best farms. A couple of special treats are roast grouse or wild Scottish turbot with champagne sauce. For the ultimate in English luxury, there's also a champagne and oyster bar to delight the finer senses. The first Royal Warrant was received in 1884 as Purveyor of Oysters to Queen Victoria, and a second as Purveyors to the Prince of Wales. Since then its dexterous team of oyster openers have won numerous awards, which include the World, British and European Oyster Opening Championships. It is situated in Jermyn Street, between St James Street and Piccadilly. John Prendergast always enjoyed dining there. He snapped out of his reverie and listened to his guest, the Editor-in-Chief of *The Guardian* newspaper.

"Yes, he's a bloody shit, that James Greene. He's rogered me well and truly!" continued Bill.

"How so?" asked John, pouring another glass of particularly fine Chablis into Bill's glass. Of course, John knew why his guest was upset but decided to play the man in case there was a snippet of extra information worth knowing.

"My K. My bloody K!" Bill exclaimed. "He promised me a K; said it was in the bag and do you know what he did?" Bill raised an eyebrow and his glass at the same time. John said nothing but merely waited. "Nothing! Absolutely bloody nothing!" Bill hissed a little too loudly at his friend sitting opposite him. John gestured to Bill to quieten it down.

Bill said, "Oh yes, sorry and all that," in a true Essex manner. He continued, "That James Greene promised me a K and then did absolutely nothing about it. My friend at the Palace knew nothing about it. The government hadn't been approached to put me forward for it and Her Majesty's Private Secretary knew nothing about it. It's a stitch up I tell you. It's a bloody stitch up and I don't know what to do about it. But I tell you this, John, I'll get that bloody shit if it's the last thing I do." He emptied his glass and John ordered another bottle.

"So what do you want me to do?" asked John Prendergast opening his hands slightly.

"Well it's obvious," said Bill. "Leak me another juicy memo so I can stitch the bastard up."

"Sorry. Can't do that Bill. We've got an external enquiry on and Mr Plod of the Special Branch is into everything, looking for moles and subversives. I've managed to point him towards a couple of women in the Case Review and Support Directorate in Fleet Street who've gone against me in the past. I've suggested an in-depth review of their security clearances with a special emphasis on their personal finances."

"Will that help?" asked Bill. "I mean, I know a little about them, remember I wrote that article? But I don't think they were earning particularly good wages, were they?"

John said, "You're quite right and that is why it looked mighty suspicious when Special Branch found that each of them was paid five thousand pounds on the two occasions when the memos were leaked."

"But," said Bill, "how did they get this money? I know that it was you, John, who gave me those memos. You actually handed them to me over a drink in Fleet Street."

"I just had a word with a friend who manages the south-east GOR for the Revenue." He saw the blank look on Bill's face and said, "The Government Office Region for HM Revenue and Customs?"

"Oh, the VAT people," said Bill.

"Exactly so, Bill. Well, I arranged for them each to receive a payment on the day after each memo had been leaked to you. I got the Revenue to pay the money through a small PR firm that we normally use for these kinds of things. Then I told Special Branch that I had suspicions about the women. Of course, the payments were discovered as were the leaked memos."

"How did they get the memos?" asked Bill.

"Simple. You know I insisted that we have a drink at the Stanley Arms in Fleet Street when I handed you the memos? Well, after we met, I went round to the Directorate and handed a colleague there a portable USB drive containing a copy of the memos in pdf format. He then simply went to each of the women's computers and loaded them into a directory. It was remarkably simple. Of course the women denied everything, as you would expect, but with the evidence of money paid to both of them as well, the Plod were far from impressed. In fact, I think the Plod is about to press charges under section 2(a) of the Official Secrets Act."

"You say that a colleague helped you? Why would he do that?"

John smiled and taking a sip of his really superb Chablis, said, "He was looking for promotion, I was looking for a favour, the two women will be sacked and our friend will become the next Assistant Director. Simple really when you think about it."

"What about the Revenue?" asked Bill.

"What about them?" replied John.

"Well, they're £20,000 down aren't they?" Bill continued, "Yes, that's five grand for each of them per memo and there were two memos. That makes £20,000."

John said, "Bill! Bill! Don't be so worried. Think it through. The Plod have found illicitly gained money and HM Revenue and Customs have a right to seize it. So it all goes round in a circle and nobody suffers."

"Except the two women," said Bill.

"Oh yes, the two women," said John. "But they were traitors after all, if not to their country, then certainly to me." He continued:

"Immigration makes many enemies."

"So, how can I get back at that shit Greene?" Bill asked.

"Well, for a start, you can't attack him directly. He's too well protected. Liam Burns is your first target; take him out and Greene is at your mercy." John paused for a moment and then continued, "What do we know about Burns?"

Bill Fillingrue-Smythe thought for a long time and replied, "Not a lot, strangely enough. He has a constituency in the East Midlands, is a Home Office Minister and tends to specialise in gambling, immigration and road safety. Seems clean as a baby's bum and is a real bastard to everyone except his friends.

He appears to be a squeaky-clean career politician and there aren't many of those around, John, as you know."

"In these circumstances, I wonder whether anybody can be as perfect as this, Bill. I'll have a word with a few friends about this chap. Do you know his feelings about freemasons?"

"He hates them, with a vengeance. He's known to be actively opposed to them at every opportunity. He's even teamed up with that fellow Chris Mulligans, you know, the MP who's being tabling all those questions about freemasons in the police, judiciary and local government. He's not popular but he's rattling quite a few cages in certain circles."

"Hmm," said John, "that should make things a lot easier," and with that he said, "Leave it with me for a week or two and I'll get back to you."

John paid the bill, they both stood and shook hands.

At that time, in another elegant restaurant in Mayfair, James Greene and Liam Burns were also deep in conversation.

Liam asked, "Any more negative press recently?"

"Not a word," replied James. "It's all gone dead. I'm worried what they're up to. I certainly don't believe we've seen the last of them. What do you think Liam?"

"I think you're right, especially with the outcome of Special Branch's recent investigation."

"Yes, I heard about that. There's no way that those two women were behind all of this. They weren't at work for most of the time and certainly didn't have access to this level of security. No, it wasn't them, that's for sure."

"I tend to agree with you," nodded Liam and continuing he said, "We've got to find out who's behind this. Now, are you sure that Robert Pennington is keeping his nose clean?" He peered at his fellow Minister.

James replied, "Oh yes, he's as good as gold. He's bending over backwards to be of help, the sycophantic turd."

"I've heard nothing from Sir Joseph. He seems to be more intent on furthering his career towards Cabinet Secretary so it's got to be someone else, someone at a very senior level."

They both said, "John Prendergast."

"Yes, John Prendergast, that smug bastard," reiterated James Greene with a large degree of venom. He continued, "What are we going to do about him, Liam?"

Liam Burns MP waited for a moment and then said, "Leave it with me for a week or two and I'll get back to you."

Liam paid the bill, they both stood and shook hands.

Strangely enough, on their way back to their offices, John Prendergast and Liam Burns bumped into each other literally; they were both trying to hail the same taxi. John deferred to Liam who took the taxi with a begrudging thank you. John's single gesture convinced Liam that the Deputy Secretary was certainly up to no good. Strangely enough, a reciprocal thought passed through John's mind. They both determined to find out what was going on.

"May I come in, Minister?" asked Sir Robert Pennington, holding a manila folder in his left hand.

"Yes, come, sit," replied James Greene to his Permanent Secretary. "What do you want? I hope it is important because I am busy."

"Well it is rather important, Minister. I think you need to be aware of this issue." Greene raised an eyebrow and Sir Robert continued, "It's bogus educational establishments; we've got about fifteen hundred of them, mainly spread throughout the south-east of the country." He paused.

James Greene sat forward in his chair and asked, "So why's this so important?" He adopted his imperious look.

"For two reasons, Minister. Firstly solving this problem would be very helpful to your Government's agenda and your own career. Secondly, this Agency has, for the first time, solved this difficult and longstanding thorn in its side."

Greene relaxed visibly and said, "OK, I'm interested, tell me about it."

Sir Robert opened his folder and pushed a report across the desk to his Minister. He said, "I'll try to be as brief as I can but it's a complex subject." He adjusted his glasses and continued, "Lots of foreigners want to get into this country and, apart from claiming asylum, the best way is to come to the UK as a student. Now, the proper educational establishments won't touch these foreigners because they can't afford the yearly fees and they don't have any academic qualifications. So it's left to shady organisations, posing as colleges of higher education, to get in on the act."

"How the hell do we allow these bogus organisations to operate like this?" asked James Greene impatiently.

"It's quite easy, Minister. Anyone can set up a college, sign a few forms and register an address, even if it is just a garage or a room above a corner shop. I mean it's so simple, even you could do it, Minister." Sir Robert realised his gaffe and shut his mouth, hoping to God, well not God because he was an atheist, but felt that he didn't want to make any enemies even if He did not exist.

He was rewarded by a higher power because James Greene, his political lord and master, merely arched his eyebrows and said, "Really!"

Sir Robert continued, "It's really quite a sophisticated process. If you are a student wanting to come to the UK, you pay a package price of about £5,000 in cash and the bogus college gives you everything, from a letter of an award of a scholarship, to a forged rent book, utility bills and correspondence from people you never knew. To all intents and purposes, you are a bona fide student who's been living in the UK for some time."

"So how do they get a passport and a UK student visa?" asked Greene.

"Both forged, probably by a bunch of criminals operating out of the East End of London. We know where they are but we leave them alone so that we can monitor them." He paused.

James leaned forward and said, "So how many students do these bogus colleges have?"

"About a thousand each," replied Sir Robert.

"And there are about fifteen hundred colleges? asked James Greene.

"About that, Minister," said Sir Robert.

"But that's incredible!" exclaimed Greene. He continued, "That's £7,500,000,000! That's nearly four times this Agency's annual spend! How is this possible? How long's this been going on?"

He glared at Sir Robert, who merely shrugged his shoulders and said, "It's been going on for as long as I can remember and I've been with the Agency for the last thirty-five years."

"Impossible! Incompetent!" exploded James Greene and sat fuming.

"But what would happen if you solved this, Minister?" He paused for a few seconds to allow his words to sink in and then pressed forward his advantage to a Minister who, for the first time, had his undivided attention. The phone rang and James snapped it up, shouted, "Not now, you cretin!" and slammed it down on its cradle.

Sir Robert continued, "And what would happen, Minister, if you were to announce this to the House?" Robert Pennington could see the visible effect his words were having on James Greene. Greene was almost salivating and probably was equally challenged by his excessive bodily functions at that moment.

The silence was broken by Greene who asked incredulously, "And you say you've solved this? How?"

"Well, it is rather simple once we introduce biometrics on exit as well as on entrance to the UK. You see, we know who all of these bogus students are, so what we do is enrol all of them in the 'Ident' fingerprint database. Once done, we put those fingerprints into the Borders Agency Watchlists so that when they try to return to the UK after their holidays back to visit their families, suddenly they find themselves barred from entry to this country. It's very much a, 'You're not coming back into the UK Mr foreigner. You don't get back into our country any more'."

"What? It's as simple as that?" asked an animated James Greene.

"Absolutely, Minister."

Greene continued, "And when can this start, Sir Robert?"

The Permanent Secretary beamed and said, "Whenever you wish, Minister. All I need is your signature on that document in front of you."

Greene searched his jacket for a pen, found none but was handed one by his official. "Do I need to read this, Sir Robert?"

"Not unless you wish to Minister," was the reply.

"It's just what you told me, is it?" asked James.

"Yes. It is substantially the same. A bit more detail I suppose. You are quite free to read the one hundred and twenty pages before you sign, if you wish."

"No point," said James Greene, snapping up the pen and signing the document, which he then pushed across the desk to his Permanent Secretary.

"My pen, Minister?" said Sir Robert just as James was in the process of pocketing it. He handed it over.

Rising and turning at the door, Sir Robert Pennington said, "Good morning, Minister."

Immigration and the Chinese

Lai Qianxian had worked for the Immigration Service for the past five years, since he graduated from Imperial College London with a PhD degree in Public Administration. He was being fast-tracked into the senior civil service.

He was just thirty-two years old and was born in Xiamen in south-eastern China. Xiamen is part of Fujian province which, owing to the mountainous landscape, is the most secluded province of the PRC in eastern China. Lai read Economics and English at Fujian Normal University, a well respected college, and was awarded a first-class honours degree. He applied to come to the UK as a student and, upon completing his doctorate, he overstayed his student visa and disappeared into the 'black economy'. He would have remained anonymous but for a random inspection by officers of the Enforcement and Compliance Directorate who raided his uncle's restaurant and found Lai and four other Chinese colleagues working illegally in the kitchens. They were all taken into custody and Lai claimed asylum. Because of his impressive academic background he was granted leave to remain in the UK. He applied to join the Government and, being highly skilled in disciplines most sought after, HM Government welcomed him with open arms and he began his graduate civil service career.

Since the late 1970s, the economy of Fujian along the coast has greatly benefited from its geographic and cultural proximity to Taiwan. In 2003, Xiamen ranked number eight GDP per capita among six hundred and fifty-nine Chinese cities, ahead of Shanghai and Beijing, while Fuzhou ranked number twenty-one (number four among thirty provincial capitals). The regional development concentrated on pure and applied technologies, such as IT, cyber cryptography and nanotechnology. In fact, it is generally regarded that about 65% of all hackers in the world reside there and practise their pan-global skills, mostly for the Chinese government but also for the province's major corporations. It is rumoured that their services are also hired out to China's bitter enemy, Taiwan, which is just across the one hundred and eighty kilometre Taiwan Strait to the south-east.

It was Monday morning, about 11.30 a.m. and Lai was returning to his desk with a fresh cup of coffee. The phone rang and Lai picked it up.

"Hello, Special Cases Directorate."

A voice said in Mandarin, "Hello Lai. It's Yang, Yang Chen, we were at university together. Have you forgotten me already?"

"Yang! How good to hear from you. How are you?"

"Very good. What about you? Have you eaten?"

"No. Where are you?"

"I'm here in London. I work here."

"How long have you been here? Who do you work for?" asked Lai.

"I work for the Embassy, have done for the last five years."

The Embassy of the People's Republic of China is situated at 49-51 Portland Place, London, W1B 1JL and its Ambassador is HE Liu Xiaoming.

Lai and Yang fixed a time to eat lunch and chose Ping Pong, a nice restaurant serving authentic Chinese Dim Sum. Only eight minutes' walk from Portland Place, they would have plenty of time to talk about old times and new developments.

When Lai Qianxian applied for asylum, his fingerprints were taken by a Livescan machine and, after a three-month process of investigation and enrolment, he was given an application registration card (commonly called an ARC) at his asylum screening interview. The card was an important document that showed he had made an application for asylum. It contained his personal details and photograph. The ARC also enabled Lai to claim financial support, a princely sum of £45 a week, which he claimed at his local post office every Monday morning. He lived with his uncle and, because he was granted a National Insurance number as part of the asylum process, he worked as a waiter in the restaurant. But that was only part of the asylum-registration process.

The Eurodac system, which stands for European Dactyloscopy, enables all European Union countries, plus Norway, Iceland and Switzerland, to help identify asylum applicants and persons who have been apprehended in connection with an irregular crossing of an external border of the Union. By comparing fingerprints, EU countries can determine whether an asylum applicant or a foreign national found illegally present within an EU country has previously claimed asylum in another EU country or whether an asylum applicant entered the Union territory unlawfully.

Eurodac consists of a Central Unit (CU) and a backup site (BCU) which includes a test system. Both are located in European Commission buildings in Luxembourg, but they are administered from the main management room in Brussels. An additional management room and a back-up storage room are located in European Commission buildings in Luxembourg. The central system connects to National Access Points via a secure network. Under the current management scheme, the European Commission, Directorate General Home Affairs, is responsible for the operation of the Central Unit of the Eurodac system, whereas the National Access Points are controlled by the relevant Member States' competent authorities. The European Commission remains responsible for the operational management of the Eurodac Central Unit, which is equipped with a computerised central database for comparing fingerprints, and a system for electronic data transmission between EU countries and the database.

In addition to fingerprints, data sent by EU countries includes:

- ☒ the EU country of origin;
- ☒ the name of the person;
- ☒ the original nationality of the claimant;
- ☒ the sex of the person;
- ☒ the place and date of the asylum application or the apprehension of the person;
- ☒ the reference number;
- ☒ the date on which the fingerprints were taken;
- ☒ the date on which the data was transmitted to the Central Unit.

Livescan is the UK's preferred method of electronic input of this information to Eurodac and so it was that at 2 p.m. on Monday 11 June 2007, Lai's fingerprints and personal information were transferred automatically to the Eurodac system in Brussels.

A week later, Li Ziranxing returned from a week's holiday with his family to his desk on the sixth floor of the general office of Xiamen Municipal People's Government at West Building, No. 61, North Hubin Road, Xiamen.

Its main functions are:

1. Prepare and arrange meetings, conferences and important activities of Xiamen Municipal Government, assist municipal government leaders to write government work reports and supervise execution of decisions made in governmental meetings and conferences;

2. Assist municipal government leaders to examine, verify and draft documents, letters and telegraphs in the name of Xiamen Municipal Government or the General Office of Xiamen Municipal Government; deal with documents, letters and telegraphs from the Central Committee of the Chinese Communist Party, the State Council, Fujian Provincial Government or Party Committee, state ministries, commissions and offices; edit and issue government gazette of Xiamen Municipal Government;

3. Handle requests and reports from district governments and be responsible for the examination and verification, thereof raise suggestions for solutions and submit for approval;

4. Coordinate disputes between different offices of the municipal government, propose solutions and submit the solutions to municipal government leaders for final decision;

5. Be on duty for emergencies and important incidents and be responsible for reports to the municipal government leaders in a timely manner;

coordinate the municipal government leaders to deal with emergencies and major accidents;

6. Inspect execution of documents issued by the municipal government and fulfilment of decisions made in meetings and conferences by the municipal government, important instructions of municipal government leaders;

7. Deal with proposals, criticisms, suggestions urged by NPC members and proposals put forward by People's Political Consultative Committee of Xiamen; report to leaders of the municipal government;

8. Direct investigation and research in accordance with instructions of municipal government leaders, report important situations in a timely manner; raise suggestions to assist decision-making by the leaders of the municipal government;

9. Collect, edit, submit and report information on government affairs so as to help decision-making of the State Council, the Provincial Government and the municipal government leaders;

10. Deal with problems raised through mayor hotline and the municipal government e-mail box; coordinate with the General Office of the Municipal Committee to solve problems raised through letters or visits of the people;

11. Be responsible for planning, construction and management of municipal government information networks; coordinate with the party and government organizations for information works;

12. Be responsible for administration of the diplomatic offices directly under the Xiamen Municipal Foreign Affairs Office and departments under the

leadership of the General Office of Xiamen Municipal Government;

13. Offer services concerning personnel, party affairs, retirees of the General Office and supervise works of subdivisions directly under the leadership of the General Office concerning offering services to personnel and party affairs;

14. Be responsible for logistic services, civil services and reception works of Xiamen Municipal Government, also the General Office of Xiamen Municipal Government;

15. Deal with other works assigned by leaders of the municipal government.

Li's team dealt with cyber espionage and, as such, he derived his mandate from function 12 above and reported to Lo Qing Lu, the Director of the People's Political Consultative Committee (Internet Affairs), which itself reported directly to the main governing body of the People's Republic of China.

Before he went on holiday, Li had instructed his team to concentrate on Italy's input security to the Eurodac system.

His thinking was two-fold:

1. Italy's cyber security was appallingly lax. In fact, its encryption algorithms kept crashing and, instead of investigating and repairing the problems, they had decided to do without. Worse still was the fact that one of their programmers had written a small script to fool the main Eurodac computers in Brussels into thinking that Italy's Eurodac satellite input and query system was operating under a full 128bit SSL encryption.

2. Italy had a particularly perverse approach to asylum, which briefly could be stated as assigning either the status of asylum seeker or illegal immigrant

solely on the basis of the nationality of the detainee. Declaring a state of national emergency enabled the Italian Government to avoid most of the EU's legislation regarding asylum and human rights. It also led to a lot of sensitive information about detainees' identities circulating freely on unencrypted government computers.

Li knew that if his team could gain access to Eurodac, then having some genuine asylum information gathered by the Italians would give the team valuable training in the use of Eurodac with a view to initiating a full-blown data mining operation. He was rewarded with success when his brightest low-level code cracker announced that he had achieved access from Italy's server by means of a series of special proxy internet servers. Proxy servers are special internet computers which hide their identities. So, for all intents and purposes, the Chinese Government could access Eurodac and it would look as if Italy were using the system. Not only that but each of the seventeen EU member states had its own country designator, Italy's being IT. Therefore, in the future, Li's team could access the data of any EU member state.

"Right, we're in sir," said Li to his superior Director Lo Qing Lu.

"Very good," was the reply. The Director continued, "Searching by country, I want a list of all Chinese people who have applied for asylum from the beginning." He signalled that the meeting was over. Li stood, bowed and left the office.

Li summoned his team and said, "I want a list of all Chinese people who are on Eurodac. Give me a list for each country. Obviously the country code will determine that. I suggest you start at the UK and then progress from there. Give me a search on *the original country of origin = 'China'* and report the name and sex of the subject and date of claiming asylum. Is that clear?" They all nodded and set to work.

"These pork dumplings are very good, don't you think?" asked Yang Chen.

"Like being at home," replied Lai Qianxian as they ate in the busy restaurant in Paddington Street.

"You want more sake?" asked Yang, draining the last of the bottle into Lai's glass. Lai nodded and Yang summoned a passing waiter.

"What do you do, Lai?" asked Yang Chen.

"I work for the Government," was the answer. "I'm in immigration."

"It must be interesting, Lai."

"It has its off and on days but, for the most part it is just boring routine."

Yang leant forward and said quietly, "Remind me which directorate you're in."

Lai's eyes opened wide as he said, "I'm not supposed to talk about it. You know that."

Yang gently took Lai's arm and said, "What kind of trouble will you get into? I've told you where I work and tell me, how long have we been friends?"

Lai sat back pondering the question. "Well it must be just over ten years now."

"Yes, ten years, as long as that," agreed Yang.

"Well, if you must know I am with the Special Cases Directorate. We handle things that don't fit neatly into pigeon-holes," said Lai.

"And I bet you liaise with some senior members from other sensitive organisations," said Yang.

"Well I do. Look can we change the subject, Yang? This is getting quite boring. I thought we were going to talk about life back home in Xiamen."

Yang said softly, "Yes, we can do that if you want." He continued, "How's your mum?"

Lai's face brightened up. "Oh, not so bad. In fact she's quite good for a sixty-year-old. She lives at home since my dad died and my sister regularly pops in to check on her."

"Yes, she did, Lai." Yang Chen sat back waiting for his words to sink in. He continued, "We had to take your mum into hospital yesterday. Don't worry. Nothing serious, yet."

Lai nearly jumped out of his chair exclaiming, "Why! What's wrong with her?"

Yang pushed him gently back into his chair and said quietly, "Nothing. Really nothing. It's just old age and she's doing fine. We're giving her the best treatment we can." Lai calmed down.

Yang continued, "And it will stay that way, provided you do a little favour for me now and again."

"What kind of favour?" asked Lai, eyes wide open.

"Oh just a bit of cyber espionage, you know, people, processes and sensitive agendas. Nothing earth shattering."

Lai started to splutter and said quickly, "I don't know about that. I mean, it's treason. I don't think I could do that, Yang."

"OK," said Yang, his eyes suddenly very hard. "Tell me how old is your sister?"

"She's twenty-two," said Lai.

"And what does she do?" continued Yang.

"She's a research student with the Department of Chemistry at the University."

"You know Lai, we have some very creative ways of destroying a person's mind. We call it a chemical lobotomy and it's done by giving the target high doses of Chlorpromazine for about a month. After that, the recipient is just a drooling, incontinent mass. Would you like that to happen to your sister?"

Lai shook his head and said nothing.

"OK," said Yang. "You go away and think about it. We'll meet here same time on Wednesday." He rose, paid the bill and left the restaurant without looking back.

Immigration and the NHS

"May I come in Minister?" asked Sir Robert Pennington.

"Yes. Yes. Stop cluttering up the doorway," replied James Greene, barely looking up from a report he was reading.

Sitting down, Sir Robert said, "I want to congratulate you, Minister, on your magnificent leadership."

"What leadership?" said James glancing up momentarily.

"Bogus educational colleges," was the reply.

"What? I'd forgotten all about them. How are we getting on, Sir Robert?"

"I am glad to report, Minister, that we have closed down about three quarters of them, barred re-entry to their students and we have achieved this within four months under your robust leadership." Sir Robert sat back, beaming at his master.

"Really?" said James putting down the report.

"Absolutely, Minister. Will you be making a speech to the House?" continued Sir Robert.

"You know, I think I may," said James Greene. "Please arrange for my Parliamentary Private Secretary to have a word with me ASAP." He buried his nose in the report again and Sir Robert left the office.

"The Minister for Immigration," announced the Speaker. He continued, "Order! Order!"

James Greene rose to his feet and started to speak. "It is with great pleasure that Her Majesty's Government can announce today that it has reduced the number of bogus educational establishments in the UK by three quarters and has prevented their fake students from re-entering the UK. That's over one million bogus immigrants thrown out of our country. This is something that no other government has achieved in the history of the UK." He sat down and a general melee of posturing and bantering ensued.

On his way out of the chamber, the Prime Minister caught his eye and he sauntered over.

"Nice one, James," said the Prime Minister. "A very good result. Keep on like this and you might have my job one day." James beamed with pleasure and went on his way with a slight spring in his step. The sun was shining in Parliament Square and he decided to have lunch in a particularly fine tapas bar in Victoria. He reached into his pocket, retrieved his mobile phone, dialled a number and said, "Yo Wanker! Fancy a bit of nosebag?"

When he got back to his office later in the day, James Greene was greeted by his Permanent Secretary who said, "I hear that your speech in the House was well received, Minister." He continued, "I have put a meeting in your diary for tomorrow morning with the Health Secretary.

"I thought it might be an idea if you two had a chat about NHS tourism by illegal immigrants. It's another vote winner."

James Greene sat back, pondering what opportunities tomorrow might bring. He said, "Very well. About 11 a.m. please. No earlier."

The next day, on the train in from Coulsdon where he lived, James pondered how the affairs of the NHS might impact upon his career. He decided not to be hasty.

"Morning James," said David Baillie, the Health Secretary. He was approaching sixty years of age, which was old for a politician bent on achieving a great office of state, but he was known as a safe pair of hands and had been handling health for the past twenty years without a major incident. "How's immigration?" he continued.

"Can't grumble," said James.

"Bit of a coup, yesterday. How did you pull that one out the hat?" asked David.

"Well, you've either got it or you haven't." James wondered where all of this was leading. He sat back and waited.

"Interested in another one, far bigger, by the way?"

"I'm always interested in well thought out opportunities," said Greene, still watching his political colleague. "What have you got in mind?"

"Health tourism," was the reply. David noted the blank expression on James's face and continued, "Let me explain. We let a load of foreigners into our country, mainly because of Tony Blair's 'big man in Europe' strategy. Well, these immigrants, mainly Indians, have very large families: mothers, fathers, brothers, sisters, aunts and uncles, who come over on a tourist visa to see their grandchildren and immigrant friends." He paused.

"There's nothing wrong with that," said James hastily.

David continued, "I know. But while they're over here, they get a bent doctor, usually another Indian, to send them to hospital to get everything fixed. These people know that if they were to get these surgical procedures done in their native land, it would cost them a fortune. So it's better to slip the bent doctor a thousand pounds a time for a free-of-charge operation at the UK taxpayers' expense. They get the operation done and are back in India before you can say Jack Robinson. It's costing the country a fortune every year."

"But don't the hospitals charge these foreigners for their health treatment?" asked James.

"Well, they try to but they are so incompetent that they do the operation first and then try to bill them three months later, by which time, they're back in India."

"But this doesn't happen in places like the USA, does it? You have to show upfront that you have the means of paying for your treatment before they'll touch you. It should be the same here, shouldn't it?"

David said, "Of course it should but our hospitals say that healing patients is their priority and the money side comes later. We've had this problem for decades, helped along by touchy-carey-feely governments, full of do-gooders from privileged backgrounds who have no concept of the practical requirements of a modern society."

"So how much does it cost the UK to treat these foreign spongers?" James asked.

"Well, the BBC did an undercover investigation last October and they concluded that the NHS had lost about £400 million in the last four years from health tourism. We actually think that the figure is very much higher than this, maybe by a factor of ten, twenty or maybe much more than this. Our view is supported by Mike Sliding, your opposition colleague for Kingswood and, as you know, he is particularly knowledgeable on this issue being a member of the Commons Select Committee on Health, specialising in healthcare reform and social care."

"I see," said James, adding, "so what are we going to do about it?"

David sat back and thought quietly for a moment. "Any chance of a drink, James?" He glanced at his watch and said, "I know it's a bit early but it's nearly noon, so that's alright."

James rose and said, "I'll do better than that. Why don't I buy you lunch? There's this little French bistro just up the road, under the flyover. They serve authentic French cuisine of the highest standard at prices that are unbelievably low – not that that matters, but you take my point?" He paused.

"I'd love to, James and maybe we could continue our discussions over this ... extended lunch."

James lifted the phone and said, "Monica?"

"Yes hi, James."

"I'm attending a meeting with the Health Secretary. I won't be back this afternoon. Please make my apologies to everyone but this meeting is my top priority, so everything else can wait." He paused to listen to what his secretary was saying and then continued, "Yes even the meeting with Sir Robert. Please rearrange it for tomorrow, not too early though. Yes. Thank you." He hung up, and grabbing his overcoat from the wardrobe near the door to his office said, "Come on, nosebag awaits us, David."

They both left Lunar House and managed to hail a taxi almost immediately.

A week later James left his house in Coulsdon, South Croydon, at 7.30 a.m. He was due to attend a meeting with the Care Quality Commission in Central London at 10.30. The Care Quality Commission runs the NHS in England and Wales and James was not looking forward to this meeting. He had little respect for these people who had, in his opinion, ruined an institution which had been an example of human compassion to the world, an institution created by the Labour Party in the best socialist tradition. And now these bureaucrats had ruined everything with their bean counters, their posturing executives, their targets and risk management strategies. And people died, in droves, from dehydration, lying in their excrement, in agony, alone and in shame. God, how he hated these people!

And no-one was held to account. No-one was sacked. No-one was charged with a crime. No-one was put into prison. *Not until now,* James thought.

He arrived at Warren Street tube station and, walking down Euston Road, he noticed how grey the air was and started to choke on the diesel fumes which belched from the constant string of buses, lorries and taxis. He looked into the eyes of his fellow commuters and saw the vacant expressions and resignations to a work-life balance that was certainly not meant to be. He stepped off the pavement and was nearly run down by a London black cab, which honked its horn angrily at him and proceeded on its way without a reduction in speed. He looked up but couldn't see the sky because of the smog; he presumed it was overcast as usual as he had been told. He looked at his notes. The meeting was to take place in the Conference Centre in the Wellcome Library at 83 Euston Road, London, NW1 2BE. He looked at his watch; it was 10 a.m. precisely. The Wellcome Library is a large building in an art deco style, on the left between Warren Street and Euston Station. Its off-white stone walls could do with scrubbing clean and its door frames could do with a coat of paint.

Sir Henry Wellcome had an early interest in medicine and marketing. The first product he advertised was 'invisible ink' (just lemon juice, in fact). In 1880, he joined his college friend

Silas Burroughs in setting up a pharmaceutical company, Burroughs Wellcome & Co. The company was one of the first to introduce medicine in tablet form under the 1884 trademark 'Tabloid'; previously medicines had been sold as powders or liquids. When Burroughs died in 1895, the company flourished under Sir Henry's leadership. He went on to establish world-class medical research laboratories and amassed the world's most impressive collections relating to medicine and health through the ages. The Wellcome Collection is now housed in the original Wellcome Building (built to Sir Henry's specifications in 1932), which is next door to the headquarters of the Wellcome Trust, his philanthropic legacy. His vision was to create a space to house his collections, where professionals could come to learn more about the development of medicine and medical science.

"James Greene, Minister for Immigration," said James to the freshly scrubbed receptionist in the lobby.

"Oh yes, Minister. You'll be here for the meeting? I'll have a colleague show you to the committee room; it's the Welcome Room."

James arched his eyebrows and the receptionist quickly lifted a phone and said, "Yes, Gareth, could you please come to the reception to conduct the Minister for Immigration to the Welcome Room? Thank you." She replaced the phone and said, "Would you please take a seat? My colleague will be here in a minute."

Ten minutes later, a colleague arrived and, apologising for the delay, tried to explain the reason for it.

"Just show me to the damned room. I'm not interested in your problems," said James Greene to the astonished minion who paused, pondering whether to protest and, thinking better of it, said, "This way please Minister."

James was shown to a modern, functional room containing a large pine table and twelve steel and wooden chairs. In front of each chair was the standard commercial pack of an A4 blotting pad, which James thought strange as no-one he knew used a quill pen and ink in meetings; well, perhaps the Foreign and Commonwealth Office might be the exception. On the blotting pad was a pencil, a ballpoint pen and a pack of post-it notes. In the corner of the room was a carafe of water and several glasses; James helped himself to some. He took his place at the head of the table and consulting his watch, which said 10.24. He opened his briefcase and placed the printed agenda and an A4 pad in front of him.

At 10.28 the majority of people, including the Health Secretary, arrived, and helping themselves to coffee, mingled until they suddenly noticed James and approached him with a view to introducing themselves. James stopped them with an upraised hand and the words, "Yes, I would like to start this meeting on time." They all settled quickly. David, the Health Secretary, introduced the Immigration Minister and invited all present to introduce themselves in turn. He turned to James and said, "Over to you, Chairman."

James thanked his political colleague and said, "Ladies and gentlemen, thank you for attending this meeting today. Item number two on the agenda. Now who has the figures?"

"May I have a copy of the agenda, Chairman? Make that two, no, three, perhaps half a dozen please?"

James arched his eyebrows and said slowly, "Did you not all receive a copy of this agenda about a week ago?" Nobody moved a muscle. James continued, "How many of you have brought the agenda with you?" Three people raised their hands. "So how can any of you have any meaningful input into this meeting when you couldn't be bothered to read and think about the issues contained therein?" No-one spoke; the question was rhetorical. James continued, "Now listen to me. When you attend one of my meetings, you will bring along your agenda, minutes of previous meetings, documents required by the agenda and you will turn up on time." Just then he was interrupted by a fresh-faced chap who entered the room, said, "Sorry I'm late," helped himself to a cup of coffee, sat down next to a buxom black colleague and started to chat about last night's social events. She nervously gestured toward the Chairman. The youth stopped, looked at the imperious, withering gaze of James Greene and repeated, "Sorry. Late again. Always in trouble."

James waited ten seconds and said, "I am the Minister for Immigration. I called this meeting and when I call a meeting, you will be on time. I am not interested in your petty and inadequate excuses for not being able to get out of bed in the morning. There are far more important matters in this world; matters of State for example. Now, have you brought along your copy of the agenda?"

"Didn't get one, sorry and all that," was the reply.

James looked at the Health Minister, his expression querying the statement. "Everyone got a copy," said David glaring at the Assistant Director. He repeated, "Everyone got a copy, even you!"

"In future, you will bring your copy of my agenda and its minutes to every meeting or I shall see to it that you are so severely disciplined that you will be lucky to find yourself emptying bins on a hospital ward when I've finished with you." A middle-aged, overweight lady with gold-rimmed, half-moon spectacles made to speak but James Greene cut her short with, "Madam, I have made an executive decision and, whereas I do not expect you or anyone else here to find it pleasant, you shall nevertheless obey it to the letter or you shall suffer severe consequences." He paused. Everyone was still and apprehensive. He continued, "I have been called in to look at this appalling situation concerning health tourism, a situation in which you as guardians of the NHS allow repeated abuse of the service by foreigners who have no right to its benefits and, judging by your slovenly approach to this meeting, it is no wonder why we have this problem arising from your governance. Well ladies and gentlemen, I've got news for you; things are going to change, dramatically and fast."

He paused and said, "I repeat my question; item 2 on your agenda; who has the figures?"

A saturnine man with a red, well-groomed beard said, "Gerald Harper, Finance Director, Minister." He passed around a three-page report and continued, "The answer to your question is not straightforward," and quickly intercepting a probable question from the Minister, continued, "for reasons I shall explain fully in a moment." He rose, and going to the white board at the end of the room asked, "If I may, Minister?" James Greene nodded and Harper continued, writing as he presented a structured definition of the charging strategy of the NHS with regard to foreigners.

He said, "Essentially, hospitals in England and Wales are obliged to ensure NHS patients have lived in the UK for twelve months prior to treatment."

James Greene interrupted, "I should think so. It would seem very strange to open the door to the citizens of the world to walk in and have free medical care."

Gerald Harper said, "Quite so, Minister, but it would appear that forty-five out of one hundred and thirty-three hospital trusts which gave details to the Care Quality Commission said they do not check. Moreover, some of the rest of those hospitals that had identified overseas visitors who had received treatment on the NHS had written off more than £400 million in losses and that, I believe, is the tip of the iceberg and I will explain in a moment if you will allow me?" He looked at the Minister who spread his hands, signalling his agreement.

He continued, "There are three major issues in my opinion. Firstly, most Primary Care Trusts in England and Wales do not check whether or not a patient is entitled to care. In most cases they assume that because a GP refers a patient to a hospital that the patient is entitled to that care. They could check but they don't consider it their job. As one hospital manager said to me, 'it's our job to heal people, not to do sums. We have accountants for that.' Secondly, there are, how can I put it Minister, a lot of bent doctors, mainly Indians, who take backhanders of between £800 and £1,000 a time to refer foreign nationals, mainly Indians again, to our hospitals. Although the hospitals seldom check, if the referral is queried then the doctor simply uses the NI number of a relative of the foreign national. There's no photograph on a health record so there's effectively no check on the foreign patient. Thirdly and finally, nearly every hospital that does treat a foreign patient waits three months or more to invoice the patient and by that time, the patient is back home in India."

"So why don't these unpaid invoices show up in the system?" asked James Greene.

"It's very simple Minister. When the invoice remains unpaid, the hospital simply deletes it from the system so it's as if no treatment were given."

James Green exploded, "What! How long has this been going on? How much are we talking about here?"

Gareth continued, "Long before I joined the Commission and your guess is as good as mine, maybe ten or twenty times we know about."

"This has got to stop. I'm not having Johnny Foreigner walking into our hospitals from his hut in the desert or hovel in some backwater city and helping himself to our world-class treatment!" exclaimed Greene.

"But we are obliged to offer emergency treatment to all people, both UK citizens and foreign nationals, if I may say so Minister," said the gold-rimmed, overweight, lady from HR.

James Greene gave her a withering look and wondered why a department called 'HR' existed; was it because its employees could not spell 'Personnel'? He assumed that was part of the reason for their perceived incompetence. He continued, "Doesn't anyone monitor these abuses?"

Jim Gove, the former head of NHS Protect, the body charged with combating fraud within the health service, called the system in hospitals 'unworkable'. He said, "The grey area hinges on the term 'ordinarily resident', which is the threshold by which people are entitled to free NHS care." He continued, "'Ordinarily resident' is a phrase which sounds like good common sense, but when it comes down to actually implementing it, the policy is often unworkable."

"This is outrageous!" said James Greene and was about to continue when a thin, forty-somethingish, mousy woman with haunted eyes and sunken cheeks interrupted with, "I am not content to progress these extreme issues. Patients have a human right to treatment without being means tested. If they come to this country and fall ill, then it is not their fault and I defy anyone to prove that they came to the UK intent on seeking treatment dishonestly. I shall not support these measures and my department will not co-operate with this vile and uncompassionate agenda." She sat back, sullenly looking at the table in front of her.

James Greene suppressed any emotion and simply asked, "What is your position and how long have you been with the Quality Care Commission?"

She turned, glaring defiantly at the Minister and said, "I am an Assistant Director with the Support Services Directorate and have been there for the last fifteen years!"

James Greene counted to ten and said softly, "As my colleague, the Health Secretary will confirm to you formally, your services are no longer required in this Commission from today. You will be paid your severance pay in accordance with your contract of service and if I receive any more insolence from you, you will be summarily dismissed for gross insubordination. You may now leave this meeting."

Mary Williams remained perfectly still, apparently in shock, as the words struck her. She made to mumble something, looked around at her colleagues for support, which did not come and quickly gathering her belongings together, fled the meeting in tears. The atmosphere in the meeting was electric.

Looking around James Greene asked, "Anyone else?" Nobody said a word. He continued looking at Gove, "So what do you need to do your job of policing this bunch of anarchic hospital trusts?"

Gove looked at the Minister suspiciously and replied, "To be blunt, I've had Ministers promise me the earth before and then renege on the deal. I don't want to go down that route again, Minister. However, I will tell you what I want and I want it in writing, if you don't mind. Firstly, I want the NHS definitions changed so that the recipient of NHS treatment is a 'human being', nothing else. Secondly, I want it to be mandatory that all hospital admittance staff must check a patient's name, address, NI number and cross-check it with the person's passport or photo ID. No treatment more than keeping the patient alive may be given until all of the checks are confirmed. Thirdly, in the case of a patient not entitled to free care, then only essential life-threatening treatment may be given until a suitable means to pay is furnished and payment taken. Fourthly, that the name and surgery of each referring doctor must be recorded and, in cases where the same doctor refers foreign nationals repeatedly, his details should be sent to my department for further investigation. Fifthly, I want the power that I should be able to hold hospital management responsible for abuse of the rules. Finally, I want a directive initiated that my department should receive weekly details of all foreign nationals treated by the NHS. That's what I want Minister."

"And what will this give this Commission?" asked Greene.

"It will give the following things minister. Firstly, it will compel hospital trusts to perform an identity check on all admissions ..."

"How will you know that they are doing this? They could just ignore the procedure?"

"Yes, they could and that is why I will have my staff attending hospitals incognito, monitoring the situation," replied Gove.

"That should do the business," agreed Greene. "I'm impressed."

"Then you will have no objection to me recruiting six undercover staff. The total revenue cost will be £300,000 a year." James Greene raised his eyebrows but Gove continued, "to save the best part of £400 million. Come on, Minister, let's put things into perspective here." James Greene was not used to being spoken to in this manner but, at the same time, he realised the sense in the statements from the security man and a synergy with its delivery.

He said simply, "You've got it! What else will it give me?"

Gove said, "My department will correlate a list of bent doctors, together with all the supporting evidence to bring criminal charges against them. The BMI may wish to take over the disciplinary proceedings and strike off those doctors and I would suggest you wait until then; it's much easier to get a conviction if their professional body itself has issued a negative ruling against them."

"OK," said Greene. "Anything else?"

"Oh yes," said Gove. "I said that these doctors are usually Indians." Greene nodded. "So, why don't we check on their status? Are they, for example, first-generation immigrants, by which I mean, did they come to the UK ten or fifteen years ago or were they born here? If they were not born here and they have clearly committed a criminal offence as I have just defined, then take them into an immigration detention centre and deport them and their families back to India."

"But, the Human Rights Act says that they have a right to family life," said Greene.

Gove studied the Minister and said slowly, "Yes it does, Minister. But it does not say in which country. You might meet opposition to deporting their families back to India but that problem is easily solved by asking the families if they want to stay here and be permanently isolated from their doctor husbands or do they want to be reunited by leaving the UK with their disgraced husbands. Put the stress on 'disgraced' to emphasise the point. In my opinion you really should have a stated policy that the UK is no place for foreign national criminals and that deportation will occur within two weeks maximum after conviction."

"I wish it were as simple as that Mr Gove," said James Greene. He continued, "You see, there is an appeals process to go through and, although we've changed this so that a deportee has only one appeal available to him or her, nevertheless the UK cannot deport anyone until this process has been exhausted."

Gove sat bolt upright and said. "Then change the law."

"What?" said Greene.

"Change the law, Minister. Where does it say in Human Rights legislation that the deportee has to stay in the UK while his or her appeal is heard? Why can't they be moved to any secure facility in any of the member states of Europe? What about detaining them in an Indian prison if they are of Indian origin? That would result in increased efficiency surely?"

Greene sat intensely listening and asked, "But how do you suggest I arrange for the Indian Immigration Service to detain these bent doctors?"

"Bribe them," was the answer. "Give them some money. Help to part-finance the budget of their Immigration Service and then invite your Indian counterpart to London and buy him the most expensive lunch and dinner you can find, put him up in the most expensive hotel in London and arrange a meeting with the Prime Minister or the Prince of Wales. It really is very easy Minister."

James Greene pondered the words for a minute and said, "Yes, I see what you mean. However, what about the rulings of the European Court of Human Rights and our own courts here in Britain when they oppose the deportations?"

"Ignore them Minister. By the time they've got their acts together, these foreign criminals will be locked up in an Indian prison with the key thrown away. I would also suggest that you repeal the Human Rights Act 1998, which has been abused by every smart-arsed lawyer in our country. I'd also like to speak with you about the ways in which we could clip the wings of these lawyers who just abuse the legal representation of foreign national criminals and immigrants but I think we've got enough on our plates with this current agenda, if I may say so."

Greene sat looking at Gove with an almost benign attitude, nay, perhaps a paternal feeling. He said, "Indeed you may. I am most impressed with your understanding of this situation and your enthusiasm to help solve it." He turned to Gerald Harper, the finance man, and asked, "Do you think these measures will solve the problems of health tourism?"

The small saturnine man stroked his red beard and said, "Probably most, perhaps the vast majority of the issues. Certainly worth implementing these measures. However, I would want a small change in the administrative processes followed by hospital trusts. I would want them to record and report to me how many foreign nationals, including their nationalities, they process every week. This will then tie up with Jim's statistics so that we will know if any hospital is fiddling the figures." He paused and then continued, "You know, Minister, we've wanted to do these things for years but we were always prevented by people from your department and from higher up in the Government on the grounds that we would have been violating people's human rights and the old chestnut that these foreign criminals were not really committing crimes; they merely had another culture which allowed these things or, and here's the classic excuse, that they did not understand English well enough to know that these things were against the law. That last excuse justified the Immigration Service spending forty million pounds a year on translators for foreigners who could speak English better than Charles Dickens. So, I'm with Jim on this."

James Greene smiled and said, "Great. Now, I'm going to pass a regulation that will make every senior hospital trust executive responsible for the actions of its trust. I shall also assume powers to be able to replace any executive with a person of my choice. I will look to you all to advise me as to who is doing or trying to do a good job and who is either slacking or obstructing our efforts." He turned to the HR lady and said, "I fear, Madam, that your department is going to be very busy in the near future."

He looked around and said, "A good result. Thank you all for attending. Meeting closed." He rose, and placing his documents into his briefcase, left the meeting room without glancing back. When outside, he dialled a number on his mobile phone and said:

"Yo Wanker! Nosebag time again. One hour, Victoria; I am at Warren Street "

Immigration and the Law

Bob Murray stood in the Arrivals Hall of Terminal Two at Heathrow Airport. In his hands he had a bunch of business cards which said, *Murray and Jones, Solicitors, specialists in Asylum and Immigration Law.* The security gates opened and suddenly a stream of multicoloured people burst forth. Some carried notices saying, 'Which way to Social Security please?', whereas others just stood bewildered, looking around but not expecting anyone to meet them. The vast majority should not have been allowed into the UK but unfortunately the shortage of resources by successive parsimonious UK governments meant that Border Control had little means of wheedling out the foreign spongers or bogus asylum claimants.

"Hello. Hello," said Bob, approaching a bunch of newcomers.

"Social security?" enquired one foreigner in broken English.

"Yes here, here," he said pointing at the address on the card.

"Is here?" queried the foreigner.

"Yes," said Bob. "You come here. You see me. Is free. I get you much money."

The foreigner looked at the card and started to smile. He gabbled away in some Arabic dialect to his friends who surrounded him and said, "Thank you much come," to Bob, who took the statement to mean that he had just acquired another dozen or so clients for his immigration law practice.

"Here," said Bob, gesturing them forward. "Bus pass," he said, giving them tokens for free travel.

"Where bus?" asked the same foreigner.

"Don't you worry, matey," said Bob "I'll show you. Come on," and calling them forward, they all set off towards the bus station at Heathrow Airport. *Right,* he thought, *we need a number* eighty-two, which helpfully was standing at its allocated stop. "Come on, come on," he said to the bunch and, making sure that each foreigner gave his bus pass to the driver, said, "Driver tell you when to get off." Bob accompanied his words with sign language and hoped they understood. He turned to the driver and said, "Drop them all off at the second bus stop in the High Street, Hounslow. I'll have one of my paralegals waiting for them. OK?" The bus driver nodded and Bob waved at the foreigners, who now seemed to number twenty.

On his way back to Terminal Two he rang his office. "Hi Linda, is David there?" David Hopkins was one of Bob's brightest paralegals. "Hello, David Hopkins," said the voice. "David, Bob. Listen I've got a bunch of twenty foreigners coming in on a number eighty-two bus. The driver will dump them in the High Street, just opposite our offices. Can you be there to meet them in, say, fifteen minutes? Yes, thanks David. Oh and by the way, can you draft in Julia and Paul to help you get them processed for emergency accommodation and also the usual emergency package of benefits? Good. Now I'm going to be here all day, at least until five o'clock. We've got another three flights coming in from Nigeria, Pakistan and Afghanistan, so we should have another fifty or so new clients today. Can you all stay late to get them all processed? We should be finished about 9 p.m. at the latest. Thanks David." He hung up.

Not a bad morning's work, he thought. *Bound to be worth a cool £300,000 unless I can increase my billings to the UK Government by thinking up a creative legal argument.* It wouldn't matter whether or not he succeeded in court; all that mattered was that he could bill the UK Government for his time at the top rate of partner.

He went to the coffee shop and ordered a double espresso. He looked at his watch and the arrivals screen. He had another fifty minutes to wait until Arkair flight W3102 landed from Lagos.

The bus stopped in the High Street and the driver said, "Come on you lot, off my bus." He gestured at the foreigners who hesitated, uncertain of what to do.

"Come on, off!" repeated the driver to the obvious dismay of the illegal immigrants.

The leader approached the bus driver and said, "Please. Where Social Security?"

This was met by a vitriolic reply; the driver said, "You bastards! You're two minutes in my country and you want bloody handouts. You can't even speak English, yet you get priority over decent English folk who've been on the housing register for years. Come on, off my bus, you bunch of fucking scroungers!" And with that, he motioned for them all to get off the bus, which then pulled away from the stop, leaving the twenty foreigners huddled in a group, uncertain of what to do next.

A young man, perhaps in his early thirties, approached them and said, "Hello. Are you from Heathrow?"

The leader showed Bob's business card and asked, "Social Security?"

David smiled and said, "Yes. Social Security." They all shook hands and David led them to his offices on the first floor of a smart, large building opposite which said, Murray and Jones, Solicitors, specialists in Asylum and Immigration Law. When they had all settled down, each with a glass of Tropicana orange juice, David asked, "Where are you from?"

This seemed to trouble them. One replied, "Social Security?" and they all agreed.

David walked to a large map of the world and pointed to various countries asking, "Where are you from?"

The leader's face lit up and he said, "I understanding." He gabbled away in an Arabic dialect, nodded to his colleagues and pointed to Afghanistan. He said, "No good. UK good. Social Security," and sat down smiling.

David said, "Well, it's not that easy and our first priority is to get you somewhere to stay and some emergency money to tide you over."

He picked up the phone and said, "Hello, this is David Hopkins, from Murray and Jones. We're solicitors in Hounslow. Yes, we've spoken quite a bit in the past. Anyway, I've got twenty asylum seekers here from Afghanistan, fleeing from the Taliban there. Can you please arrange some emergency accommodation for the next couple of weeks while you process their claims? OK good, thank you. Oh, when will the transport be here to collect them from our offices? About an hour, maybe half an hour? Can you also arrange for the driver to have twenty emergency benefits packs with him? Yes, I'll sign for them. OK thanks, bye." He put down the phone.

"Now," he said to the refugees, "each of you has to sign this document." He distributed one copy to each of them.

The leader looked up and asked David, "Is what?"

David looked down at him and benignly said, "Social Security," and pointed to where the leader should sign. He then went around the others pointing to the same place.

Two seemed to refuse to sign but the leader explained, "They no write."

David sighed and said to one of the illiterates, "Thumb here," and demonstrated thereafter signing his own name and applying his firm's stamp to confirm that he had witnessed this claimant's application. He collected all of the forms and said, "Here, rub this on your fingertips." He gave them each a tube of superglue and pretended to demonstrate. "No! Don't close your hands. Just let the glue dry. Open your hands like this." He showed them.

The converted Ford Transit van arrived from the local Enforcement and Compliance Office ten minutes later and the sight of official uniforms seemed to unnerve the foreigners. "Police," said the leader and they all started to run from the offices.

"No, no," shouted David. "Social Security. Money. Here look!" They turned to look at David, holding £40 in his hands. He gave the money to the leader who looked at it, turning the notes over and over, then smiled and gabbled something in a foreign language. His colleagues immediately crowded around David who gave a welcome emergency benefits pack to each of them.

"Social security," they all chanted with obvious delight.

One of the Immigration Officers was heard to mutter, "Bloody fucking spongers! I'd shoot the lot of them if I had my way."

"And I'll have your job if I hear any more of that racist language," roared David. He continued, "These people have rights. They are fleeing from nightmares of violence that the likes of you can't even imagine. Now, take them to their emergency accommodation and if I hear any complaint from them, I promise I shall have you disciplined."

He turned to the leader and said, "All of you. ASU, Croydon, tomorrow. I will be there at 10 a.m." And, turning the Immigration Officers he said, "Right, I want all of them at the Asylum Screening Unit, Lunar House, Wellesley Road, Croydon at 10 a.m. tomorrow sharp. Understand?"

The surly one said, "We do know where the ASU is, sir."

David quickly countered with, "Yes, but I don't want you taking them to the ASU in Liverpool and then complaining that I didn't tell you which one, Officer."

The claimants left his office and David completed his time sheet. He was encouraged by the partners to bill his time at £120 per hour, in six minute tranches, and he always billed double the time he spent on the legal aid cases. He consulted his diary and calculated that he had billed an average of ninety-six hours a week. That would mean that he would receive a monthly bonus of just over £4,600 before tax. He sat back and thought how much he enjoyed his work.

Adeola Adindu got off Arkair flight W3102 from Lagos and was met by Bob Murray in the Arrivals Hall of Heathrow Terminal Two. Bob handed him a business card which said *Murray and Jones, Solicitors, specialists in Asylum and Immigration Law.*

"You fleeing persecution?" he asked.

"No," replied Adeola. "I'm looking for a job."

"What?" said Bob. "You've got a work permit and a visa?"

"No," said Adeola. "But I've heard it's easy to just walk in and get one. I've just walked straight in now. I said I was a tourist and they stamped my passport for three months."

"You can't do that, matey," said Bob.

Adeola's nostrils flared as he said, "Don't you oppress me, Mr White Man. I am not your black slave!"

Bob put a hand on the big Nigerian's chest to stop him walking away and said, "Now you listen to me, son. There's ways and ways of doing things and your way will land you in prison. I know because I am a lawyer. Now, if you follow my advice, you will get what you want and it'll all be legal. So, do you want to listen or do you want to keep insulting me?"

The Nigerian thought for a minute and replied, "OK, so I will listen to you."

"Right," said Bob. "Now where are you from?"

"From Nigeria of course. From Lagos."

"Well that's no good," said Bob. "You'll be deported the moment they catch up with you. You'll have to come from somewhere else. I know. You're from Somalia and you're escaping torture and certain death at the hands of the Islamic rebels. You've seen them kill many people in your village and you can also say that they raped and killed your wife. Yes, that should do the trick."

Adeola said, "But why would I say these things?"

"Because you are claiming asylum, son. That's why. If you say you come from Nigeria, they'll have you back there in no time because there's no violence there and therefore you can't claim asylum."

"But why do I want to claim asylum?" asked Adeola.

Bob looked him straight in the eye and said, "For an intelligent man, you're not really streetwise are you? I'll spell it out for you. The reason you want to claim asylum is to receive free housing, free money, free healthcare and to be able to work in the UK. Now for that to happen, you need to be a person fleeing from persecution and the nearest place to your home is Somalia. Right?"

"OK."

"Right," said Bob. "Have you got a passport on you?"

"Yes. I have my Nigerian passport," said Adeola.

"Give it here," said Bob. "You don't want the authorities to find that on you."

"But I will need that," said Adeola.

"No you won't. Well, not for a long time and when you do, we'll get a forged one from some people I know in Commercial Street in East London. As a matter of fact, they specialise in forging Nigerian passports. Takes about a day or so to get a new one. Oh, and make sure it's not dated the day before you want to leave."

"Why?"

Why?" exclaimed Bob. "Why? Because who would have a brand new Nigerian passport dated yesterday when he would have been in the UK for the previous two weeks on vacation? God's teeth."

"Oh, I see," said Adeola.

"Now, what language do you speak?"

"English, naturally. It is the first language of Nigeria. I also speak Igbo, which is the leading dialect of my country."

"Well, you're going to have to speak Somali. No best say nothing. You could always say that you speak Bravanese or Bantu but, knowing your luck they would bring in an interpreter who could speak these languages. Yes, best to say nothing. Just shrug your shoulders, that should do the trick."

"Right now, here's your tube of superglue." Bob handed it to Adeola.

"Why do I need superglue?" he asked.

"To remove your fingerprints. Rub the stuff on your fingers at the ends and it will burn off your fingerprints. That way they won't be able to fingerprint you. In other words without a passport and fingerprints they won't know who you are, will they?" asked Bob.

"But how long does it work?" asked Adeola.

"About six months to re-grow your fingerprints. That's why you should keep an eye on them and, if it looks like they're re-growing, put another dollop of superglue on them."

Bob gave him a bus pass and said, "Out of that exit, turn left to the bus station. It's a number eighty-two bus. Ask the driver to drop you off at the second bus stop in the High Street, Hounslow. I'll have one of my paralegals meet you there and take you to our offices. Best of luck. Sorry I have to go," and, with a shake of Adeola's hand, he rushed off to confront a large group of foreigners.

"Social Security?" he asked, handing each his business card and a bus pass.

Immigration and Travel Documents

"Good morning, Minister," said Sir Robert Pennington, entering the office with a small manila file in his hand.

"Good morning, Sir Robert," said James Greene feeling in top form that morning. "What's new?"

"Quite a bit, Minister. There are quite a few areas which could do with your expertise, in my opinion."

"Hmm? What areas?"

Sir Robert opened his file and slid a single A4 sheet across the desk. As the Immigration Minister read it, Sir Robert said, "I would advise that you pay a visit to the Travel Documents Department. It's only up the road and I think it will be an eye opener for you. Anyway, it's somewhere to start. I've arranged a meeting for you to see Simon Schuster, who leads the department at 10.30 a.m.; that's in about twelve minutes' time."

"What's the agenda?" asked Greene rising from his desk.

"Just leave it to me Minister. I think you will be amazed at what you hear," said Sir Robert, closing his manila file.

They left Lunar House and, turning left, walked up Wellesley Road for four hundred yards. They entered a grey, faceless building and, after signing in, were conducted to the sixth floor where they were met by Simon Schuster, who was the Country Manager for the Country Returns Operations and Strategy Directorate.

"Please sit down, Minister," he said, gesturing towards one of the pine and steel affairs that grace so many offices in the public and private sectors. He offered coffee, which was declined, and then asked, "What can I do for you?"

Sir Robert quickly interjected, "I believe that your department is solely responsible for obtaining emergency travel documents for the UK's failed asylum seekers and foreign national criminals once they have served their sentences in UK jails. Is that right?"

Simon rubbed his chin and said, "Well, the Foreign and Commonwealth Office, both here and abroad is involved and, of course, we must remember all of the Foreign Embassies and Consulates but I think I can say that we, in this department, co-ordinate it all." He sat back, beaming with satisfaction.

"So, please remind me how many cases you are currently handling?" asked Sir Robert.

Simon quickly consulted his desktop computer and said "168,412, Minister."

"From what date?" Sir Robert asked.

"Emmm, 2011. No, April 2010. Yes, that's it."

"What about before that?" asked Sir Robert.

"I don't have the precise figures I'm afraid. We have moved offices many times in the last decade. I would say we moved every eighteen months or so and we had four changes of computer systems, each of which did not talk to the other. So, I'm afraid I don't know the answer to your question, Sir Robert."

"OK. Approximately how many cases have you had since, say, 2005? Just an approximate figure."

"Approximately, I would say about 700,000 cases, maybe a few more."

"And did you manage to obtain emergency travel documents for all of these cases?"

"Good God no. Nowhere near it," replied Simon.

The Minister was about to open his mouth when Sir Robert kicked him quite forcibly on the leg. He continued, "What percentage would you say obtained Emergency Travel Documents? Just approximately."

Simon rubbed his chin again and said, "During that period it was very difficult for us in this department. You see, the Government's policy was very different to now. Foreigners were encouraged, if I may say so, to come to the UK and there were so many levels of appeal against asylum decisions that it could take years for us to arrive at a situation where the asylum claimant's appeal process had been exhausted. And then, we would face an administrative action from the claimant's legal representatives under the Human Rights Act; you know, a right to family life and all that."

"So what approximate percentage did you remove?" repeated Sir Robert.

"Well, during that period, I would say something like 7%."

Sir Robert glared at James Greene who was about to say something and didn't. The Permanent Secretary then smiled at Simon and said, "And if I understood you correctly, there were approximately 700,000 cases during that period." He took out a calculator and said, "That means that approximately 49,000 were deported; let's call it 50,000, shall we? What happened to the other 650,000 people?"

"I don't know Sir Robert. We couldn't find many of them and even those who were in prison, we had to let go because the process was taking too long and we were violating their human rights, you see."

Sir Robert smiled again and said, "But some of those foreign national criminals that you let go were very violent. I mean there were quite a few murderers, rapists and robbers, weren't there?"

Simon nodded and said, "I believe so, but what could I do? Our lawyers said that we were violating the prisoners' human rights. We had to let them go. The process was taking too long."

"So why was it taking so long, Simon?"

"Well it's the same nowadays. In a nutshell, if we want to deport anyone, I really should say *administratively remove* when it comes to failed asylum seekers, we have to obtain travel documents from their home countries before they are allowed to travel. Now that may seem easy but most of these cases have burned off their fingerprints using superglue. The majority was never fingerprinted when detained, so we don't know who they are or where they came from. Now, to complicate it, they often lie about their origins. For example, if they've come to the UK illegally from Nigeria, they will claim that they come from Somalia and are fleeing from persecution. We had a case just last year where we were convinced a chap came from Mozambique, so we put him on a plane at Heathrow. When he landed, Immigration at Mozambique said, 'he's not one of ours', and put him back on the plane to London. We got hold of him and put him back on the plane to Mozambique and they sent him back to us. I had to contact one of our Foreign Ministers who had a word with our Ambassador over there who, in turn, I believe told his counterpart in the Mozambique Government that their President could forget about 'borrowing' a tranche of the UK's next foreign aid payment to his country and our man over there suggested that the President might have to cancel his daughter's wedding because of a lack of funds to pay for it. I believe the matter was solved and Umbikee was repatriated to Mozambique the next day."

James Greene sat red-faced as if he were about to explode.

"Is it always like this?" asked Sir Robert.

"Oh far worse, usually. China and Vietnam are far, far worse than this. Oh, they appear to be models of co-operation but they are as bent as a nine bob note when it comes to repatriation. We've got an agreement with them; it's called Operation Elucidate. Under this agreement, they are supposed to come to the UK three times a year to interview cases where we think they are Chinese or Vietnamese nationals. Well, they come here once a year and talk to the claimants and then usually say that the addresses and names given by the claimants are clearly non-existent and, therefore, they won't issue emergency travel documents to these people. We get lumbered with them and, if we keep them locked up or detained for more than a year, their lawyers sue us for violating their clients' human rights. However, if we let them go, they disappear into the UK's black economy, never to be found again, unless it's six years later, in which case we have to grant leave to remain in the UK because they've been here for too long to be removed under the Human Rights Act."

James Greene asked quietly, "Who pays for all of these legal fees?"

"The UK, Minister. It's all done on legal aid and there's no cap on how much each case costs nor on how much a lawyer can charge in respect of his hourly fee. It could be as little as £50 an hour for a solicitor in a small practice but it could be as much as £5,000 a day for a Leading Counsel like the ex-Prime

Minister's wife. And you've got to remember that Leading Counsel must always have a Junior and be instructed by a Senior Partner, who is a solicitor, who would be assisted by another solicitor, two paralegals and a gofer. So you could be spending about £15,000 a day on some of the high profile cases like Abu Hamsa, the hook-hand cleric, and look how long that went on for. And the thing gets worse. All of these big legal teams raise argument after argument and our small legal team can't keep up with it all. You see, it doesn't matter whether or not the other side would win these arguments in court. It's just that we don't have the resources to argue them all and, as a result, courts give them a default judgement. We just can't win, Minister."

"But is there nothing you can do?" Greene asked.

Simon shook his head and said, "There's nothing I can do but there is something you can do if your government wants to solve this situation." James Greene sat bolt upright in his chair and Simon continued, "You could cap the hourly rate of all lawyers working on legal aid cases to a maximum of £75. Don't get me wrong, I'm not saying that you should cap legal aid, that would be illegal under European Law, but you could limit the hourly rate any lawyer, solicitor or barrister of any rank could charge to a maximum of £75 an hour."

James Greene interrupted, "But wouldn't this disadvantage asylum seekers. I don't want to be the one accused of preventing Johnny Foreigner from pursuing his bogus asylum claim because of a lack of funds to pay his lawyers with."

"No, no, not at all, Minister. All I'm talking about is placing a limit on the lawyers' hourly rates. You can get a damn good solicitor or barrister for £75 an hour, believe me. And, if Leading Counsel or Senior Partners want to take on these cases, then they could always do them at the same hourly rate;

there's no-one preventing them from taking on the cases, we're just limiting how much they charge the State."

James Greene sat silently for a moment and then asked, "And if I do this, what's likely to happen, in your opinion?"

"Apart from protests from the Bar Council, the Law Society, the BBC and the left-wing press? Nothing! Except all of these high-priced lawyers who have been on the gravy train of immigration fees for over a decade would go off and try to rape and pillage other areas of legal representation. I predict it would happen within three months of you changing the system, Minister."

James Greene looked at Sir Robert and they both said, "Interesting."

On Tuesday, the following week, *The Guardian*'s front page figuratively screamed:

'Government stops legal aid to the most vulnerable.'

It continued:

'The Guardian has just learned that Immigration Minister, James Greene, has changed the law so that asylum seekers and other vulnerable members of our community are now unable to obtain proper quality legal representation. Imagine, if through no fault of your own, you are fleeing your village to avoid torture and death and on arrival in the UK, your lawyer says to you that he can only work a couple of hours per week representing you; what are you going to do? You can't go back to your country and you can't get justice here in the UK. This is another example of the shameful policies of our infamous Immigration Minister. It is a sad day when things have come to this.'

It was signed: Bill Fillingrue-Smythe, Editor-in-Chief.

The phone rang and James Greene picked it up. "Hello?" he said.

"Minister, its Simon Schuster. Thank you for changing the law. I have some good news for you. Over the past ten weeks, we have had just over 150,000 letters of resignation by our claimants' legal representatives. Now we shall be able to clear the vast majority of these claims very quickly."

"How?" asked James Greene.

"By entering requests for default judgements against all of the cases where the claimants have no legal representation. It's not our job to find them lawyers and, if they haven't got any, well, we can't hold up the judicial system until they get some. It's really bloody marvellous, if you'll pardon my French."

"So, how quickly can you have them out of the UK, Simon?"

"Ah well, it's not that simple, Minister. You see, we still have the problem of getting emergency travel documents and the biggest problem is that these failed asylum seekers don't want to leave the UK for some grotty hovel in the middle of a desert. If you can solve that, I'll have them out of the UK within a month."

James Greene said goodbye and hung up. He understood that prison space was very limited in the UK and, even if he had a budget for building detention centres, these bloody human rights lawyers would not let him bang up foreigners to rights willy-nilly. He had a thought and dialled a number.

"Justice Commissioner's office. How can I help you?" asked a delicately modulated female voice.

"Paul Souveryns, please. James Greene, UK Immigration Minister."

A few minutes later a voice said, "James! How good to hear from you. How's everything?"

"Good Paul. Tell me something, are you interested in controlling a bit more of Europe's justice system?"

"Of course I am, James. Do you want me to take over your job? Not up to it, eh?"

"Calm down, Paul. I want to know something. Do you know how many prisons and detention centres there are throughout the EU? More importantly, do you know how full or empty they are?"

The Commissioner said, "No I don't but why do you ask, James?"

"Because Paul, the UK has got tons of failed asylum seekers and foreign national criminals and we've got no prison space. So we have to release them and that just encourages more to come to the UK. Now I was thinking, if you could get your people to knock up a computer system which would monitor all available space in the various EU member states, then I could send over a bunch, say, 150,000 of my lot to a prison you recommend, say, in Romania. We would be willing to pay a certain amount to the Romanians for the use of their facilities. What do you think?"

Paul thought for a moment and then said, "Yes. I think that could work, after all there would be no challenge from the European Court of Human Rights because we are all civilized in Europe. When do you want this by?"

"As soon as possible, Paul. I've got a crisis here."

"OK, leave it with me. I'll make it top priority. It doesn't seem a big problem. We might have something in place within three months. Good to speak with you."

James hung up, reflecting on the reality of the situation. If this scheme worked, he could remove failed asylum seekers and foreign national criminals to a jail in Romania, which would not be the bed of roses it was here in the UK and he was very certain that these lying claimants would soon remember where they originally came from when faced with the prospects of years in an ex-Soviet Romanian prison. If they did that then Simon Schuster would get emergency travel documents for them and they would be out and back to their bloody hovels in a desert. The word would soon get round that other bogus claimants should not come to the UK for fear of being locked up in Romania or Bulgaria. He chuckled and thought maybe they'd go to France instead.

He felt good.

Six months later he addressed the House.

"Mr Speaker, it is with great pleasure that I can announce the following facts about immigration. In the past six months we have removed 187,534 failed asylum seekers and some of the most violent foreign national criminals from the UK. During the same period, new claimants for asylum have fallen from 35,000 per month down to 5,850. This is the lowest number of asylum claims recorded for any administration and I am pleased that this Government has proved that it is serious about immigration into the UK." He sat down, and Members on his side of the House rose as one and applauded him.

Immigration and Private Healthcare

Vajubhai Advani was fifty-seven years old; it was his birthday and all around him were gathered his extended family. Many had travelled from their homes in Chorvad, Gujarat Province in India. His ancestors had lived there since the eighth century when, as Parsi Zoroastrians, they had fled from the Muslims in Iran (as it is now called). Vajubhai had come to the UK over forty years ago with his father Nitin, who owned the world's largest ship breaking company situated at Alang near Bhavnagar. Vajubhai's father was a powerful man back in India. He had served as one of the one hundred and eighty-two members of the legislative assembly of Gujarat and had personally known Mahatma Gandhi, also a Gujarati, during his campaign for independence from Britain in 1947.

The state of Gujarat is situated in the north-west of India and is bordered to the north by Rajasthan; to the south by Maharashtra; to the east by Madhya Pradesh and to the west by the Arabian Sea and the Pakistani province of Sindh.

All present were vegetarians and considered this to be the healthiest cuisine available to anyone even, it was said, promoting long life and health. As he sat listening to a group of musicians playing Gujarati folk music, which is called Sugam Sangeef, his mind drifted back to the days of his childhood when his father would take him to the beach to fly his kite every December during the festival of Makar Sankrati. The heady music from the mixture of wind, string and percussion instruments conjured up the rising and falling, the swooping and diving of his ornate kite dedicated to the deity. Here in his substantial home in Little Chalfont in Buckinghamshire, he felt at one with the world.

He ate another vegetable pakora and suddenly collapsed.

The next thing he knew was waking up in The Cotswold Hospital in Little Missenden. This was one of the many BPC Healthcare hospitals throughout the UK and it specialised in providing private healthcare to its patients. Its main specialisations were complex surgical procedures not normally found elsewhere. It was not a big hospital, only having fifty-five bedrooms but each offered privacy and the comfort of en-suite facilities, satellite TV and telephones. Caring and professional medical staff, with dedicated nursing teams and resident medical staff on duty twenty-four hours a day, ensured the highest possible support to any patient.

"Mr Advani. Mr Advani. How are you feeling?"

Vajubhai Advani opened his eyes and croaked something unintelligible.

"Don't worry, Mr Advani. You're in hospital. You're quite safe. My name is Mr Narenda Solanki. I am the Senior Registrar. I specialise in gastroenterology and I'm looking after you."

Advani nodded to show that he understood.

The doctor continued, "I hear that you had a problem at your birthday party. Well, we'll soon have a little look at why and get you back on your feet. OK?" He turned to Mrs Advani and said, "Nothing to worry about. It may be just a heart murmur but we'll soon find out once we do some tests. By the way, where are you from originally?"

Mrs Advani said, "Gujarat State."

"So am I!" replied the doctor. "But I left there over fifteen years ago, after I qualified in my specialism. Well, as I say, we'll soon know what's wrong when we've done some X-rays and blood tests. I wouldn't like to speculate at present but I don't think you should worry at all." He turned to Mr Advani and asked, "Are you quite comfortable, sir?" Advani nodded and the doctor said, "OK. I'll go and prepare things. In the meantime, I'll leave you in the hands of Senior Nurse Henderson," and, with a reassuring squeeze of Mr Advani's hand, he left the private cubicle.

The tests took about two hours and the doctor returned, his face much more serious this time.

"What's wrong, Doctor?" she asked.

"I don't know yet, Mrs Advani. I'm going to do some more tests on Mr Advani's liver. There's something not quite right about it. It's not functioning at 100%. Anyway, I am going to keep him in overnight while we do these tests. I should have the results by noon tomorrow and we can then decide where to take things. Now, we have facilities for you to stay; nurse here will show you. Please order some food and wine; we have an extensive menu. I would, however, prefer if Mr Advani stayed off food. Some orange juice is fine but no solids and certainly no alcohol. It would interfere with the tests. Now, is there anything else that I can do or tell you?"

"He is going to be alright isn't he Doctor?" asked Mrs Advani anxiously.

"Of course he is. He's in the finest hands here. Don't worry. We'll know everything in the morning. You go and get a good night's rest."

When she'd gone, Mr Solanki looked down at his sleeping patient and, stroking his chin, thought, *there's something seriously wrong here.*

Govinda Patel was fourteen years of age; in fact it was his birthday. He lived on the streets of Mumbai and had ever since he could remember. He could just about remember his mother. She had done her best for him ever since his father had left but eventually she was forced into prostitution, earning what little she could by selling her body to anyone who had money. She was killed eight years ago when a client had strangled her as he approached orgasm on their 'marital bed', which was a suburban rubbish tip. It was then that Govinda decided to go on the streets, working every scam under the sun and using his wits to make a little money here and a little money there. He survived.

One day, he heard that the local hospital was advertising for organ donors. Apparently, it was paying good money. He learned this from one of his friends who could read and write, well, after a fashion. He carefully remembered the address of the hospital and the name of the doctor. He set off to find out more and, who knows, maybe make himself a fortune. He arrived at the hospital and asked to speak to the doctor. The nurse clearly did not approve of Govinda and told him to wait in a corner and not to sit down on the clean chairs in reception. She went away to find Doctor Kapoor. After forty-five minutes Doctor Kapoor arrived and the nurse pointed out Govinda.

"What do you want?" asked the small, tubby doctor, about forty years of age.

"I want some money," replied the boy.

"Get away from here with your begging, boy! This is a hospital, not a Buddhist temple," said the doctor angrily.

"But the newspaper said that you wanted donors and would give money," answered Govinda. He did not know what the word 'donor' meant but he knew it paid money and that was all he cared about.

"You want to become a donor?" asked the doctor. Govinda nodded and said he knew many other friends who could do it if the money was right. He thought that this 'donor' might be something to do with sex, probably helping older men to get an erection but he didn't care, so long as he got paid for his services.

"Alright," said the doctor. "I will have to examine you and perform some tests on you before I agree to anything. But first, you must have a bath because you are filthy and smell to high heaven. Nurse, take this boy and make sure he bathes thoroughly. Then give him a sterile gown and burn these clothes."

The nurse screwed her face up at the sight of the wretched boy and commanded, "This way, dirty boy."

After Govinda had bathed and had each part of him inspected by the nurse, he was given a surgical gown, which he put on. "This way, dirty boy," said the nurse, who led Govinda back to a sterile, non-descript cubicle in the A&E Department.

Thirty minutes later, Doctor Kapoor swept aside the curtain and, checking off the document on his clipboard, said, "Right, let's have a look at you."

He started with an examination of the skeletal structure, ensuring that the boy had healthy arms, legs and a straight back. He next looked at the boy's eyes, teeth and ears. "Ever fallen over a lot or got dizzy?" he asked. Govinda nodded his head negatively. "Here, drink this," said the doctor. It was a white liquid which tasted of nothing really. The doctor then went over to a kidney tray which was resting on a small filing cabinet and, picking up a hypodermic syringe, said, "I am going to take some of your blood for analysis. It won't hurt. Turn your head away." The doctor took two syringes full and labelled them for different ranges of microbiological and histological laboratory tests. "Right, it's off to X-ray with you." The doctor told the nurse to take Govinda along to the X-ray Department, on the same floor. "Get them to give him a general MRI scan. I want a spinal X-ray and a soft tissue CTC scan of his internal organs and his brain. Tell me when the results are in; I'll be around."

The nurse said, "Come with me, dirty boy."

The next day, Mr Solanki asked Mrs Advani to sit down on a chair next to her husband's bed. He took a deep breath and said, "Look, I shall not beat about the bush. I must tell you straight what we have found. It's not good. Mr Advani, your liver is beginning to fail. It has already lost 60% of its functionality and it won't last much longer. You have extensive cirrhosis of about 40% of the important parts of your liver and I regret to say that your condition seems to have resulted from a very high alcohol intake over a prolonged period of time." Mr and Mrs Advani looked at each other; they both knew that he had a drinking problem of many years.

The doctor continued, "The prognosis is very bad, I'm afraid. You need a complete liver transplant and, if you don't get one, you'll be dead within three months." Mrs Advani suddenly let out a cry and burst into tears.

"But you can do the operation, doctor. You are a specialist in gastroenterology, aren't you?" asked Mr Advani.

"I am indeed Mr Advani and you need have no worries about my ability to perform this operation. However, the problem lies in finding a suitable donor. I had a look on the UK register this morning and there are no donors available. There is a man in Newcastle-upon-Tyne who was involved in a bad car crash two weeks ago. Now, he might die within the next few weeks but, up to now, he's holding his own in Intensive Care. So I can't make any promises to you. It would be wrong of me to give you false hopes."

"But does this mean that my husband is going to die?" asked Mrs Advani.

"Without a suitable donor, I'm afraid that it means precisely that. There are no donors in the UK. Now that might change tomorrow, but I cannot say that for certain," the doctor replied.

"But what about in other countries, maybe Europe or the USA or India?" asked Mrs Advani.

The doctor placed a hand gently on her arm and said, "I don't know and even if there were a liver available, we would have to move very quickly, and it would cost a lot of money to pay for the operation on the donor and then to transport the liver here before it suffered any damage."

"Then do it, Doctor. We have money. We can pay any price. You must save my husband!" she exclaimed, looking at her husband, who simply nodded.

The doctor rose and said, "I'll make enquiries. I'll do my best. In the meantime try not to worry." He left the private room intent on making an international phone call to his friend in India.

"Doctor Kapoor, A&E, good evening, how can I help you?"

"Nirmal is that you?" asked Narenda.

"Yes. Who's that?"

"It's Narenda. Narenda Solanki. Don't tell me you've forgotten me already?"

"Narenda, how good to hear from you. How's gastroenterology?"

"Not bad. Keeps me in booze and cigarettes. How are you doing in A&E, Nirmal?"

"OK, I suppose. It's always busy and I've often thought of giving it up and joining the private health gravy train like you, you devil."

Narenda laughed and said, "It's not a bed of roses. We do have some problems from time to time, I can tell you. That's really why I wanted to talk with you. I've got a patient with chronic cirrhosis. He's got about three months to live and obviously needs a liver transplant. Unfortunately the UK transplant bank hasn't got any spare livers so I thought I would ask if you've got any."

There was a moment's silence and then Doctor Kapoor said, "It's strange that you should ask me that because only today I got a suitable donor in. Now, I haven't completed the tests yet but the liver looks OK; it's not been damaged in any way and it has the normal signs of functionality. It would certainly be worth investigating."

"No time for that Nirmal," said Narenda. "I need it over here as fast as possible before it starts to degrade."

"Oh there's no danger of that; the patient is still alive."

"What, he's perfectly healthy?" asked an incredulous Narenda.

"No. No. He's on his last legs but, at the end of the day Narenda, you've got to ask yourself whether or not you want to save your patient. So, what is it? Do you want the liver?" There was a silence for about a minute after which Narenda asked, "How much?"

Doctor Kapoor paused and then said, "Well I'd want five thousand for the liver; that's five thousand US dollars, not rupees, Narenda. Then there's two economy tickets by Air India from Mumbai to London Heathrow; one way in the case of the donor. There'll be an overnight hotel stay for the person accompanying the donor and a nice meal and some wine or alcohol. Then if you want to give me something for my trouble, that would be nice of you, Narenda."

"How much in total, Nirmal?"

Doctor Kapoor took out a calculator from the top right hand drawer of his desk and eventually said, "Fifteen thousand US dollars, including my fee of 20%. It's very cheap and it's available now."

Doctor Narenda Solanki stared at his desk. This was totally unethical but, on the other hand, he felt he owed a duty of care to his client who, quite frankly, had no chance of survival otherwise. He asked, "When can they travel, Nirmal?"

The answer was, "Tomorrow, 10 a.m. local time. Be with you at Heathrow, say 2 p.m. your time. Can you arrange an ambulance to meet them? OK, give me the name and address of your hospital for immigration purposes."

Narenda did so and said, "Thanks Nirmal."

Doctor Kapoor interjected suddenly, "Hang on Narenda, before you go. Do want any other parts? I mean, you've only had his liver and there are plenty of other organs in tip-top condition. How about his heart, for instance? Tell you what, I could do him as a job lot for another fifteen thousand on top of this deal. What do you say?"

"I'll think about it. Good to talk with you, Nirmal. Bye." Doctor Solanki hung up and sat looking at his desk. Yes, he had saved his patient's life but at what cost? He got up and poured himself a cup of coffee from the Kenco coffee machine just inside the door to his office.

The next morning Doctor Narenda Solanki visited Mr Advani. Mrs Advani was also there and it was obvious that she had been crying. They both looked up as the doctor entered. He decided to put on his brightest face.

"I've got some good news for you. We've found a liver in Mumbai. It belonged to a young lad who tragically died in a car crash in the city centre. It's being flown over this morning and should arrive in Heathrow just after lunch. I'll have to do some preliminary work on it to make sure everything's functioning properly but, barring any problems, I would expect to take you up to the theatre about 4 o'clock this afternoon. Is that OK, Mr Advani?"

"I'm most grateful, Doctor," he replied.

Mrs Advani clasped the doctor's hand and asked, "My husband will be alright, won't he?"

Doctor Narenda Solanki smiled benignly and replied, "Don't you worry, Mrs Advani. I've conducted this type of operation over a dozen times and I've never lost a patient yet. Of course your husband will be OK and you'll be able to see him at about 8 o'clock tonight. Now he won't say much because he will still be under the anaesthetic and he will look a little yellow but that is perfectly normal in a liver operation. Now, I must get on to prepare; it's going to be a busy day."

He smiled and left the room.

Govinda was excited as he sat with an older man in the departures lounge of Chattrapathi Shivaji International Airport at Mumbai. He'd never been to any foreign country, let alone the United Kingdom and he was looking forward to it. Wait 'til he told his friends about his adventure.

He didn't know what it was about but the older man said that they would only be away for a couple of days, a week at the most. Govinda thought that it might be a very wealthy man who wanted a pretty boy for sexual purposes but he didn't mind. He had been told many times that he was a very handsome boy and he would do whatever the UK man wanted to achieve sexual satisfaction. He knew many techniques from Karma Sutra, although he could not read and his friends had told him that he must use his techniques to make the man's penis hard as quickly as possible in order to make him orgasm. Once done the man would leave him alone and Govinda could count his money.

Just then an announcement was made for flight AI 192 and the man said that they should go over to the departure gate. Govinda watched the man hand over two boarding cards and his passport. He heard the flight attendant ask if the boy was his son. The man replied that Govinda was his son and that he was going to London for medical treatment. They were shown through and were soon seated in seats 42 a and b. Govinda fiddled with air vents and lights and the old man stopped him, saying that they would be thrown off the aircraft if they caused any trouble.

After fifteen minutes they taxied out to runway 27 and, having checked with Air Traffic Control that the intersecting runway was clear, Captain Peter Martin released the full throttle of the four engines of the Boeing 747-400, which surged forward like a giant gradually gaining speed. It took off and Govinda, who had the window seat, was amazed to see the ground falling away below him. Clouds enveloped the plane and after what seemed like an eternity to Govinda, the plane punched its way through the clouds, which now appeared below like a sea of cotton wool.

The stewardess came around asking if they wanted drinks. The older man ordered a double gin and tonic for himself and an orange juice for Govinda. Govinda was absolutely fascinated by everything. He even took one of the flight magazines from its pocket in the back of the seat in front of him and, although he could not read, he found great delight in looking at the brightly coloured pictures. The stewardess returned to take their order for the main in-flight meal. The man ordered two vegetable curries with rice, naan and pickles and asked Govinda how he was feeling. "OK," said Govinda and the man sat back dozing. There was nothing for him to do for the next eight hours.

Doctor Narenda Solanki finished his conversation with reception. The private ambulance had arrived and Narenda said he would be right down. "I'll need you with me Nurse Henderson. We're off to Heathrow to pick up a liver donor for Mr Advani's operation this afternoon." They both hurried down to waiting ambulance.

Two hours out of London Heathrow, breakfast arrived: vegetarian breakfast for both of the passengers. The man felt in his pocket for the little phial that he had been given by Nirmal Kapoor. *What was it the doctor had said to me?* the old man asked himself. *Empty all of this into his food an hour or two before you arrive at Heathrow and then just say that an ambulance is waiting to take the lad to hospital to try to cure him of a rare illness. And then you return to Mumbai the next day.*

"Govinda. Why don't you go to the toilet? You haven't been since we left Mumbai and I don't want you peeing down your trousers before you meet our wealthy sponsor." Govinda rose and went to the toilet at the back of the aircraft.

Now alone, the old man emptied the contents of the small flask into Govinda's tarka daal and mixed it in well with Govinda's fork. He sat quietly eating his vegetarian madras.

"Excuse me," said Govinda on his return and the old man said, "Here you sit at the aisle; I will move up. Here's your food. Eat it all up; it's expensive so you must not waste any." Govinda was hungry. He was not used to having so much good food and he needed little encouragement. He polished off his plate and sat back smiling. About an hour later the Cabin Services Director announced, "Ladies and gentlemen, please return to your seats, stow away your tray tables, place your seat-backs in an upright position and fasten your seat belts. We are on final approach to London Heathrow Airport."

These were the last words Govinda ever heard.

"We must be allowed to go airside," said Doctor Narenda Solanki. "We're meeting a young boy who is arriving from Mumbai on flight AI 192."

The Airport Security man examined the documents given to him by the doctor and looking inside the ambulance said, "OK Doctor, just wait here and I'll have a truck guide you to the aircraft." In less than five minutes, a truck with a sign on the top saying 'Follow Me' appeared at the security gate and set off with the private ambulance in pursuit, headed towards flight AI 192.

"Help somebody!" shouted the old man in seat 42a. "He's very ill," he said.

The Cabin Services Director arrived and asked, "What seems to be the trouble sir?" She looked at the young Indian boy who was clearly unconscious, very pale and appeared not to be breathing.

"He's here for treatment at a hospital. He's very ill. Please, there should be an ambulance waiting for him. Please check, miss," said the old man desperately.

The Cabin Services Director picked up a phone and spoke to the Captain. A few minutes later, the Captain confirmed that there was an ambulance waiting on the tarmac at the rear of the aircraft. He ordered a ramp to the rear and announced, "Ladies and gentlemen, I would ask you to stay in your seats. We have a small technical problem which we are resolving. It shouldn't take long and then you'll be free to go."

The ramp came and the two ambulance men carried Govinda onto a stretcher. Once in the ambulance, Doctor Solanki and Nurse Henderson started to couple drips and to remove some of Govinda's clothing in order to attach the wires to an electrocardiograph but, within minutes, the flat-line trace indicated a total lack of life signs in Govinda's body.

"He's dead," said Narenda to his nurse, who agreed with her doctor's diagnosis.

Back on board the plane, the Cabin Services Director spoke to the old man. "Was he a friend of yours, sir?"

"No, I hardly knew him. I spoke a few words to him and this seemed to be his first trip to the UK. He said he was looking forward to it and telling his friends back home. He also told me he was ill and that he had been told that an ambulance would be waiting for him when he landed here. That's how I knew."

The Cabin Services Director said that it must have been a shock for him and asked if she could do anything to help him. He answered no.

"You see, I hardly knew him," said the old man, collecting his hand baggage and heading towards the exit, intent on a night on the town on full expenses.

It had been a good day.

Doctor Narenda spoke to the ambulance driver. "Come on. Hurry up man. I've got to keep this liver fresh. Use your blue light, for God's sake."

They were back at The Cotswold Hospital just over half an hour later, and Dr Solanki jumped out of the ambulance and asked, "Is Theatre One prepared? Right, let's get him up there at once." The doctor went immediately to Pre-Ops and, removing his jacket and shirt, scrubbed up to his elbows with Acriflavine, an orange, antiseptic scrub and, having dried his hands, placed them into rubber surgical gloves. His Theatre Sister helped him into a surgical gown and placed a mask around his face.

"Let's get to work," he said picking up a number 20 Swann Morton scalpel.

At fifteen minutes past eight o'clock, a visibly exhausted Dr Solanki entered the Pre-Ops reception room and, conducting Mrs Advani to a small meeting room, said, "He's going to be OK. The operation went like a dream. You can see him now, if you want. Nurse will show you to the ward."

"Oh thank you, Doctor," said Mrs Advani clutching at his hands. She said, "You must feel so good, saving so many people's lives."

Solanki hesitated and, remembering all that he had done in the last twenty-four hours, had a slight bowel opening, to his acute embarrassment.

Immigration and Europe

"So what will you do if our courts just ignore your rulings?" asked His Honour Lord Richard Johns QC GCMG of Berkhamstead.

"But you have no choice," was the reply from Paul Souveryns, the EU Commissioner for Justice. He continued, "It is the law." He paused. "You should know this Lord Richard; you should know the law."

"I do know the law, Paul. After all, I have made my career in that discipline. But I repeat my question."

Paul shifted in the seat of his high-backed black leather armchair and, gesticulating impatiently said, "But your courts are subservient to the various European courts of justice both in the Hague and Strasbourg. Your laws are made there, not in London and we also supervise your competence in the decisions your courts issue daily on matters which are presented to them. This is an undeniable fact. Your courts need to learn about these things." He sat back smirking.

"With the greatest respect, Paul." Richard sat back waiting for the obvious reaction to his insulting statement and, when he observed a vacuity in his opponent's behaviour, he sadly understood the limited ability of European officials to engage in rhetoric effectively and on a subtle basis. He continued, "The earliest vestiges of European constitutional law stem from the ratification of the European Convention of Human

Rights in 1951, a convention that you and your European counterparts were either too lazy or too incompetent to write for yourselves. It was the British who wrote the convention and now, by a freak occurrence of pan-political connivance, fuelled by greed and egotism, you have been placed in a position of power that is neither deserved, understood nor permanent. You dream about a Most Serene Republic of Venice and think you can, so easily, reincarnate the most boring city of Brussels into a similar exalted state, not from global trade and finance but from stifling bureaucracy and posturing. Your ideal of reform is the issue of another two hundred page report on the required size of a carrot – hardly the stuff empires are made of."

He had seldom seen an EU Commissioner apoplectic but his words seemed to have hit the right place with this boring official. He rose and said, "The time for talking is over Paul. Her Britannic Majesty's Government has decided to redefine its policy concerning immigration and Europe." And with that he left the post-modernist office on the twelfth floor of the EU Commission's offices in Brussels.

"I'm announcing a referendum on the UK's membership of the European Union," said the Prime Minister to his Cabinet colleagues.

"Do you think that is wise?" asked his Foreign Secretary.

"Yes, I do. Why?"

"Are you serious that you are going to let the British people decide on whether or not we stay in Europe?" asked the Chancellor of the Exchequer.

"Sort of. Why?" replied the Prime Minister.

"Because," replied the Chancellor, "they will vote no. Overwhelmingly. Without a shadow of a doubt. I think the current polls show that 77% are in favour of leaving the European Union."

"Exactly! And is this common knowledge, would you say?" The Prime Minister looked at the sea of bewildered faces. None said a word so he continued, "Do you think they know this in the European Commission?" Most nodded. "May I ask you, my most trusted colleagues, for your advice on this subject? But before I do so, let me explain this to you." He rose and started to pace the ornate room like a senior lecturer delivering a thesis.

"Would you all agree that the Commission, not the Council of Ministers or the European Parliament has too much power and exercises too much unaccountable influence over Britain, its trade and its constitution?"

The Secretary of State for Trade and Industry said, "Absolutely Prime Minister, without a doubt." He turned to his colleagues around the table, acknowledging a sea of nodding heads, like flotsam in a multi-coloured foreign lagoon.

The Prime Minister smiled gently and asked, "And do you think that our leading partners in Europe feel the same as we do? After all, it is we, the leaders of the developed countries in Europe who should be deciding all of these things, not some unaccountable, faceless, incompetent junior Ministers who could not win power in their own countries' general elections and instead seized overall power of the Commission because there was no process to prevent them doing so. They act solely in their own interests, not in anyone else's. It does not matter if countries are going bankrupt, if a country's leaders are grossly corrupt, if a country's farmers are inflating their figures concerning the number of sheep, cattle or wine production; it does not matter to them if they know that most of the financial awards they grant find their way into the Swiss bank accounts of First Ministers and their senior Cabinet colleagues. They know all about this and they don't care so long as their Commissions increase in size and command larger and larger annual budgets. Money and political power are all these people want." He paused and all nodded their agreement.

"I've been in touch with my German counterpart and she is of the same opinion. I've also been in touch with my French counterpart and, despite him following a very different economic agenda, he is also in agreement with me in principle. The same is true for Spain, Portugal and Italy, as well as the northern states. I have not consulted Greece because I think they have their work cut out dealing with their current problems. I also hear that our small cartel wants Greece out of the euro but is being prevented by the Commission, so I've suggested a way forward on that issue also."

He picked up the carafe of water before him and pouring some into his glass, took a long pull at it.

He continued, "So, I've played a trump card. I have stated that the UK will have a referendum on EU membership. I know that the Commission knows that the British people would vote overwhelmingly to exit the EU as it stands. In fact, only last night, at about 11 p.m., I got a call from that snake Paul Souveryns, asking, no nearly pleading with me, to change my intention to offer the referendum. I told him I was powerless to change people's minds given the bureaucratic structure and governance of the EU by the Commission. He asked me what I meant and I told him that I was committed to offering the British people a choice about membership of the EU but what they would be voting on would be a European Union at that time. He began to understand. I said I wanted widespread repatriation of powers, like sovereign powers over our waters and fishing rights; like sovereign rights over our immigration policy without interference from the European Court of Human Rights; like absolute control over our financial services and the independence of the City of London; like free trade with our European partners without the interference of the Commission; like a reduction in our contribution to the EU budget in line with the annual budget minus the contribution made to the Common Agricultural Policy; like an embargo on European Nationals having free access to our labour and social security markets; like foreigners having no right to repatriation to their country of origin at the UK taxpayers' expense for the purposes of having their babies."

"And what did he say?" asked the Chancellor.

"He paused for a moment and said that he did not see a problem; as long as I could persuade my German and French counterparts, anything else would be a bonus."

"And can you?" asked the Chancellor.

The Prime Minister beamed, "Of course. Where do you think this agenda came from? The UK, Germany, France, Spain, Portugal and Italy, together with some touchy-carey-feely Nordic states, will all renegotiate their membership in accordance with this agenda. Too long has the Commission ruled us; now they will become what they should always have been, a bunch of typists and accountants with the real power vested solely in the Council of Ministers." He paused and then said:

"That's what the British people will vote on."

He sat down and looked around.

Five Cabinet members actually applauded the Prime Minister and I think it is true to say, though no-one can know the thoughts of another, that each Cabinet member recognised the sheer genius of their leader.

"It's brilliant!" exclaimed the Foreign Secretary. "You've given the Commission no choice. If they said no then the referendum would overwhelmingly result in the exit of the UK from the EU and they would never allow that. This way, they agree to all our demands and we vote to stay in. Brilliant!"

"But what would have happened if the Commission had said no and we voted to exit the EU?" asked the Secretary of State for Trade and Industry. "We would really be in the poo then, wouldn't we?"

The Prime Minister gave him a withering look and said, "You really must give me some credit, Geoffrey. Our German and French counterparts had envisaged this and we would have evoked contingency plans to ensure we enjoyed the full benefits of membership while outside the Union. After all, even the Commission cannot afford to lose the UK's annual contribution to its agenda of private jets, private palaces, worldwide holidays and the whole gravy train of obscene privileges and corruption." Everyone smiled except Geoffrey, who blushed. realising his gaffe.

"I'm not really sure if this is a measure for the better," said Roger Delavigne, his senior Commissioner.

"It was the best I could do, given the situation and I do not see a problem," replied Paul Souveryns to his boss.

"I disagree and I disagree most strongly. What you fail to realise is that once this kind of thing starts, then it might spread to other member states and result in total ungovernable chaos. I am not content with your handling of this issue, Paul." Roger leaned back in his chair arching his eyebrows at his junior.

"That is most unfortunate Roger because you are wrong. What you fail to realise is that we administer all of their money. We decide who gets what, when and how and, if we run out of money, for whatever reasons, we just ask them for more or regrettably refuse to finance their pet projects. We find that staff are unavailable for things like the translation of minutes of their key meetings; that transport is unavailable for their travel to venues on fact-finding missions; that funds are unavailable to pay their grossly inflated expense accounts. There are hundreds of ways to bring them under control. We control the money and the means and therefore, we are in total control." Paul Souveryns looked imperiously at his boss, daring him to take the next step, which he did.

"I don't agree and I am calling a meeting of the whole Commission to examine this matter!" He expected Paul to quake before his words. He was wrong. Paul simply said:

"Go for it, Roger." And leaving his boss's office, turned at the door and said, "May the best man win!"

The Commission met a week later and both Roger and Paul made their cases on the issue. The Commission thanked them both and two hours later dismissed Roger Delavigne to his total amazement.

"We've been looking to get rid of him for some time," explained the President of the European Commission to Paul whom he promoted. "Well done, Paul. A nice pragmatic solution in our opinion." He patted Paul on the back and then left for a meeting on the fate of the embattled euro.

Immigration and Scotland

"I've done it! I've finally done it!" gloated Kenny Herrings as his victory in the Scottish elections was provisionally confirmed at 4 a.m. on a grey, dismal day in Edinburgh.

They had all been against him and his vision for a Scotland that, under his governance, would be a free sovereign nation, free from the yoke of English tyranny that had crushed the ancient kingdom of Alba for over four hundred years; a kingdom of noble Malcolm, of Margaret the Saint, of the warrior king Robert the Bruce and of the legendary William Wallace, the scourge of the English king and his French queen. They had taken its gold, cleared its peoples, robbed its oil and sold its fish. They had taken all and given back a pittance. But no longer. Kenny would change all that or die in the task of trying.

There was a knock on the door of his Cabinet Room in Bute House and in came a diminutive dark-haired lady of about fifty years of age. "It's great, isn't it? You've done well, Kenny."

"We've done well, Mary," he answered. He looked at his political colleague Mary Roe, MSP for Glasgow Eastside and who undoubtedly would become his Deputy First Minister of Scotland.

It hadn't been an easy election; the folks in his Aberdeen North constituency were traditionally staunch Scottish Socialists but two things had launched him to power with a landslide majority in the 2011 Scottish elections. Firstly was his ceaseless energy in campaigning for what he believed to be right for a free and democratic Scottish country rather than a backwater province of a Labour-run Westminster Government. Secondly, he was helped into power by a new Labour party which, neglecting its grass roots in the working-class shipyards of Glasgow, now favoured the politically correct, openly corrupt bankers of Edinburgh. The election results said it all; the SNP totalled sixty-nine seats, Labour had thirty-seven, the Tories had fifteen, the Lib Dems won five, and others totalled three. He had said to the Scottish people, "I'll govern for all of our ambitions for Scotland and all the people who imagine that we can live in a better land. This party, the Scottish party, the national party, carries your hope. We shall carry it carefully and make the nation proud."

He believed every word of it and was proud that his nation felt the same.

A deeply religious man, he still found time to attend the Church of Scotland every Sunday at St Giles Cathedral in the high street in Edinburgh before taking a pint of foaming sixty shilling ale in Deacon Brodies pub, slightly to the left and opposite.

Bute House has been the official residence of the First Minister of Scotland since 1999. Located at No. 6 Charlotte Square – the north side of the square – it is reckoned to be one of the finest examples of Georgian architecture in Edinburgh. It is next door to the Georgian House, No. 7 Charlotte Square, a public museum run by the National Trust for Scotland. Bute House is distinguished from the outside by its four pilasters under a central pediment. The drawing room is used for welcoming visiting dignitaries to Scotland, for press conferences and ministerial receptions. The dining room is used for more formal occasions such as state dinners.

The land for No. 6 was sold in 1792 by a public group to Mr Orlando Hart, shoemaker, for £290. In 1806, Sir John Sinclair, Bart. of Ulster, bought the house for £2,950. The house was sold again in 1816 and a little over a century later. Having changed hands several times, it became the property of the fourth Marquess of Bute. In 1966, the house, together with Nos. 5 and 7, were conveyed to the National Trust for Scotland in lieu of duty on the estate of the fifth Marquess who had died in 1956.

The vestibule of Bute House is unusual in Robert Adam's design for Charlotte Square in having a central front door. The present entrance hall was designed in 1923 by the architect Balfour Paul for the fourth Marquess. It is in the Adam Revival style with a central chimney piece in white marble and elaborate stucco decorations. It forms a small lobby leading to the staircase.

Bute House staircase consists of cantilevered stone steps that would normally stop at the second or bedroom floor, with a cupboard-like arrangement of wooden stairs continuing to the attics. The uppermost flight at Bute House was probably added in 1889 by the architect Thomas Leadbetter, at the request of Sir Mitchell Thomas of Cammo, a Lord Provost of Edinburgh who wanted a billiards room on the top floor to take advantage of the spectacular views of the Firth of Forth. The staircase dome with its festoons of decorative plasterwork may be original.

The drawing room's plasterwork ceiling is original. Its geometrical design and neo-classical ornament are a restrained version of Adam's own ceiling designs, but with the lightness of touch and delicacy that characterises the styles of the 1790s.

A portrait of the third Earl of Bute, new single doors in the Adam style replaced the double doors that once joined this room with what is now the Cabinet room. A new chimney-piece with a central tablet depicting Venus and Cupid and vases echoing the frieze were also installed. The continental glass chandelier is one of three Bute family pieces now in the care of the National Trust for Scotland. The full-length portrait on the north wall was painted by the artist Allan Ramsay and shows John Stuart, third Earl of Bute (1713-1792), the first Scottish-born British Prime Minister.

The Cabinet room was originally a library or private study. This room now hosts regular meetings of the Scottish Ministers.

The dining room retains its original late Georgian cornice but is otherwise a recreation by the fourth Marquess in 1923 when the sideboard recess was formed. In 1966 the Bute House Trustees commissioned the suite of reproduction mahogany ladderback dining chairs, which are based on the eighteenth century originals at Penicuik House. The dining table was designed to match these and suits the narrow proportions of the room. The mirror over the fireplace was made for the drawing room at Duff House in Banffshire circa 1760 and is attributed to a cabinet maker called Mackie, then established in London, but who may have had family connections in the north-east of Scotland. The Millennium Collection of modern silver, which is often displayed in the room, was commissioned in 1999 to promote the quality of Scottish craftsmanship. It was fashioned by fifteen of the country's top silversmiths to coincide with the return of a Parliament to Scotland after three hundred years and was presented in June 2001. It is on permanent loan to the First Minister.

"We're going to change this country, our noble Alba, for the better, for the first time. The English do not understand us; how could they? They are a foreign nation, more German than anything. They don't realise that we are an ancient nation, as old as theirs and we don't need our hands held when it comes to governing ourselves. I have a vision for us, Mary, a sovereign nation playing an increasingly powerful part in a federal Europe of like-minded countries, united in commerce, in currency, in mutual defence, mutual wealth creation but with our separate and complementary traditions which enrich each other's development. For the first time, Scotland will have its independence with the security of more than two dozen European allies, united into federal unification." He leaned back in his red leather chair and looked at Mary, his deputy.

She gazed at him with the look of love clearly in her eyes. She had loved Peter for many years, ever since she had first seen him speak in Aberdeen. He was magnificent when he addressed a crowd, even a hostile crowd because, whatever one thought of him, Peter came over as a most sincere man who firmly believed in what he said. He had never been known to lie, which was unusual in a leading politician and, perhaps most importantly, he had a way of predicting the future – what he said usually came to pass. He was also a deeply religious man, attending church every Sunday, not for political effect, but because it seemed to refresh his soul. More than this, Mary thought, he always had time for the ordinary man, the man in the street, whether the most educated or the least capable. She noticed that whether or not they sympathised with his political views, they nevertheless respected him and left with a favourable view of the man. Maybe that was why he was so popular in the polls, thought Mary. He certainly seemed to be winning his case for Scottish independence and it seemed that there was nothing that the major political parties in Westminster could do to resist his progress towards his innermost political desire.

"We're going to win," said Mary Roe, placing a hand on her boss's, and would-be lover's, left shoulder.

"We're going to lose," said Liam Burns, who had been appointed by the three major political parties to lead the counter-offensive against Scottish Independence from Westminster. Liam had been chosen partly because he was indirectly descended from Robert Burns, the Scottish poet, but mainly because he was a formidable political fixer. "He's the best man for the job in my opinion," said the Chief Whip for the Conservative Party; his view was confirmed by his counterparts in the Socialist and Liberal Democratic parties.

"We're going to lose," repeated Liam to a sea of smug faces.

Immigration and Religion

"Bless me father for I have sinned. It is two days since my last confession. I did my penance and received absolution. I accuse myself of belittling a newspaper editor who was criticising one of my Government colleagues."

"But why did you do such a thing, Liam, my son?" asked Monsignor Peter Morris, the Chaplain at Netherhall House, one of the male-only halls of residence for Opus Dei.

The answer was, "Because he was opposing my Minister for Immigration who, in turn, was endeavouring to do God's will in this matter."

"I see," said the Monsignor. He continued, "and did it give you any pleasure to see the editor humiliated by your actions?"

"No, Father, it did not. I merely obeyed God's voice in this matter."

The Monsignor thought for a moment and then asked, "Liam, what do you mean by 'God's voice'?"

"It is a voice within me, that speaks to me clearly every day and I obey Him whose voice it is," said Liam Burns with a burning conviction of veracity.

"But how do you know it is the voice of God? Could it not be your own voice or worse still, that of the devil, Liam?"

"No, Father. I am sure it is He, who made me and all living creatures."

"Liam, I have no doubt that you follow the teachings of Our Lord Jesus Christ with a most commendable zeal but I would caution you to be careful with regard to these voices in your head. You must know that Satan and his hordes have many most devious ways to mislead us and infiltrate our souls in our constant battle against the legions of the dark."

"I understand you, Father and humbly ask for your forgiveness and a severe penance for my sins and ignorance."

Father Peter Morris sighed. He had been the Chaplain for Netherhall House for the last fifteen years and seldom had seen such a religious fervour in any Opus Dei numerary. He resolved to speak with his Bishop James Herrington, the Auxiliary Bishop of Westminster, about Liam's vocation at the earliest opportunity. He was worried that there was something distinctly unhealthy about the whole thing.

He said, "Liam, for your sin, please say three Hail Marys but, to stop Satan from misleading your innocent soul, I order you to wear the Cilice for two hours every day, that you shall endure the whip every day for fifteen minutes, that you shall take a cold shower every morning and evening for a week and that you shall practise a denial of your choice at meal times also for a week. These voices are the legions of Satan, Liam, and you must be rid of them before they possess you. I now absolve you of your sins by the Father, Son and Holy Ghost. Go in peace my son."

Liam rose and entered the body of the Church to perform his penance.

Liam Burns was a numerary of the Order of the Opus Dei, that is he was a celibate member of the Order who lived at one of the centres, in this case, Netherhall House, in Hampstead, near central London. In fact the hall of residence backed onto Hampstead Heath, itself just 5.7 miles from the Houses of

Parliament where Liam spent most of his days. Many times he had wanted to become a priest and thereby become a member of the Priestly Society of the Holy Cross but always his worldly duties prevented him from doing so. Having said the three Hail Marys, he retired to his sparsely-clad room and, opening the right-hand door to his wardrobe, he retrieved his Cilice, a band of steel about six inches in width with vicious barbs embedded into it. Having strapped it to his left thigh, he felt the barbs bite into his flesh and the ensuing fire of pain start to cleanse his filthy body of its corporal desires. He wiped the sweat from his face and knelt to pray to God. When he had finished his supplications, he walked to his bathroom where he kept his flail. This was a thick cord, about two inches in diameter, into which Liam had embedded strong industrial staples which would rip flesh from his buttocks when he flagellated his dirty body. He used to whip his back until a colleague at one of the Select Committees upon which Liam served, remarked that Liam had marks of blood on the back of his shirt. Liam was forced to tell the lie that he had scraped his back on gravel while servicing his car. That little lie saw his buttocks red raw in that evening's confession. He slept on the floor, without a blanket. Morning came quickly and Liam jumped up to attention and then performed one hundred prostrations to his God of salvation. He shaved and showered in icy cold water, dressed in his best Crombie suit and denied himself breakfast.

The journey from Netherhall House to the House of Commons was a mere 5.7 miles and should have taken him twenty minutes. Invariably it took an hour, sometimes more. He turned out of Elm Row onto the A502 and was glad to see only a little traffic. It was 7 a.m. and the sun was rising gloriously in the east. His praises were short-lived because he met three incidents immediately upon turning right onto the A400 towards London Euston and Kings Cross.

Incidents! he thought. *Bloody road works, that's what they are! Two weeks ago the Gas Board dug up the road to cure a leak. Then the Water Board dug it up again, in exactly the same places to stop a leak. And then, if that was not bad enough, the Electricity Board has just dug up the same three holes to install fibre optic cables. Why can't they dig the holes once and then do all of their work together?* he asked himself. He resolved to speak with his counterpart at Transport.

He drove on through Holborn, Marylebone and Westminster to his reserved parking place in Parliament Square. There had been fifty-six 'incidents' in total on his journey of a mere 5.7 miles. He prayed his prayer of vengeance against Transport for London would be answered by his God. He entered the Members' Entrance in the northern part of the west façade and proceeded north from the Central Lobby, which is the crossroads of the Houses of Parliament. He walked the length of the Commons' Corridor to enter the Members' Lobby, wherein Members often hold negotiations and where accredited journalists lobby senior members of the Cabinet or Opposition. Although originally built in a style mirroring the Peers' Lobby, the damage sustained during the 1941 bombing was not repaired in places, the most notable being the Rubble Arch, the entrance to the Commons Chamber, which most people wrongly call the House of Commons.

Liam Burns passed this entrance, which is flanked by the bronze statues of Winston Churchill and David Lloyd George, the Prime Ministers of the Second and First World Wars respectively. He rubbed the feet of these statues with his hand in the established tradition observed by most MPs. He climbed two sets of ornate stairs and arrived at the corridor which led to his office, at the end, on the right.

"Fucking arseholes!" he exclaimed to his colleague, the Member for Northampton, who shared his office and political views.

"Bad journey in?" enquired Bernard Chalk.

"I swear they do it on purpose, Bernard. It can't be that difficult to get all of these utility providers to coordinate their public works and thereby minimise disruption to the public. Can't we fine them every time they dig up the same hole? Surely there must be something we can do to stop them disrupting the traffic in London. It must be possible to improve our journey experience, reduce pollution from standing vehicles stuck in traffic jams and also save money."

"I know, old boy," said Bernard, "but the trick is to make them play ball. They are very much a law unto themselves. I would suggest you have a word with John Wilson; he's an up and coming light in the Division of Traffic and Infrastructure. I believe he's the Deputy Director of that part of Transport for London and I know for a fact that he's greedy for power."

Liam paused for a moment and, stroking his bald head, said, "Is that a fact?"

"Yes it is," said Bernard, "but you'd better get some big guns behind you because he'll need a lot of support to change the opinions of his dinosaurian colleagues. Be especially careful of the executives of London Underground. They are the power behind the throne and they will be your biggest opponents."

At the same time Kate Jones, a Labour rising star, was seated behind her desk on the third floor of Portcullis House, which is that strange chimney-shaped building across the road from the Houses of Parliament. She, too, did not smoke, drink or take the name of her Lord God in vain. Like Liam, she was a fervent member of Opus Dei and also lived in a hall of residence. Unlike Liam, she lived in the Ashwell House residential hall just off City Road in N1. Opus Dei, a Roman Catholic institution founded by Saint Josemaria Escriva, ensures that men and women numeraries of the Order always live separately. It is sincerely felt that the unnatural stirrings of the flesh, which proceed from Satan and his hordes, would only be aided by close interaction of men and women of the Order who, as numeraries, are all celibate. It was felt that separation of the sexes was good for the contemplation of the higher values proceeding from God and his Blessed Son by the power of the Holy Ghost to manifest themselves in daily life opportunities. Liam and Kate sought to turn every moment of their daily work into moments for growing closer to God and for improving society. They met at conferences and seminars and had growing respect for each other and their bonds in the Order of God.

Kate rose and walked to the window overlooking Parliament Square. She wondered what Liam was doing at that moment.

At that moment Liam was storming back and forth cursing, in a quite graphic manner, about what he would like to do to a Deputy Secretary in the Home Office. "Those insignificant tykes over in the Home Office have made James Greene's life hell, you know?" he said rhetorically to his colleague Bernard. "James is alright but he's not exactly switched on to these bastards. He keeps walking into their traps. You know I had to threaten John Malthouse with an external investigation into the leaking of Government papers before he started to take me seriously. The pompous, privileged shits!"

"Nearly lunchtime," said Bernard. "You for a bite and a small tipple?" He looked at Liam's imperious glare and said hurriedly, "Sorry, old fruit, I forgot. You don't drink and all that stuff do you?"

Liam said, "I do not drink alcohol. I find that it clouds the judgement and leads to the most abhorrent behaviour." The phone rang and Liam answered it. It was his Monsignor.

"Can you meet me this afternoon, Liam? No, the lobby will do. I want you to meet someone. It's very important."

They agreed to meet half an hour later.

"Something important?" asked Bernard.

"I don't think so. It's just an old friend who wants to talk to me about something religious."

"Oh, I see. Not really my cup of tea, Liam. For a minute I thought you'd decided to sneak off for a small snifter with a lady friend." The look that he received made Bernard Chalk quickly exclaim, "Just a joke, Liam. It was just a joke, nothing more!"

Liam studied his colleague and said slowly, "It was not in the best of taste, Bernard."

"No. Well. No. Maybe not. I'd best go. See you after lunch or whatever. Sorry." And with that he left the office.

Monsignor Peter Morris was on time and he and Liam shook hands firmly.

"Liam, my son, how are you? I'm glad you could meet me. It's something very important. I want you to meet someone." He led Liam out of the Saint Stephen's public entrance and hailed a taxi. "Westminster Cathedral please driver," he said and they both sat back in silence. On arrival at the Gothic church off Victoria Street, they were met by Father Joe Evans, who led them to an office on the second floor. This, the office of the Auxiliary Bishop of Westminster, was as ornate as its occupant, Bishop James Herrington, who beckoned them both to comfortable armchairs in the corner. No refreshment was offered. The Bishop began, "Liam, how long have you been an MP?"

"Just over thirty years" was the reply.

"And how long have you been a senior member of this country's Cabinet or that of the Opposition?"

"A good twenty-five years I think."

The Bishop leaned forward slightly and said, "Yes, you've done well for yourself, that's for sure."

Puzzled and nervous Liam said quickly, "I hope I have done good for others and followed the teachings of God, your Excellency."

Gesturing towards Peter Morris, the Bishop said, "That would be our view as well." He paused, looking carefully at Liam and then continued, "How long have you been a numerary of Opus Dei?"

Liam thought for a moment and replied, "I think for all of that time. I really wanted to become a Deacon of the Order and then be ordained but daily circumstances have repeatedly stopped me from being a useful servant to our Order. Don't get me wrong, I have endeavoured to help the Order in various ways over the years ..."

"Yes Liam, I know you have. For example, you founded the organisation 'The Way of Christ'." Liam nodded. "And how much has it raised for the Order would you say?"

"I don't know precisely but at a rough guess I would say close on fifty million."

"And have you been successful in recruiting upstanding and highly respected members to our Order?"

"Yes, your Excellency. I have recruited just over a thousand members from the City of London: leading bankers, solicitors, brokers and several politicians such as my good friend in Christ, Katherine Jones."

"Yes you have been a loyal servant of this Order and a model member of this Holy Church. You know Liam, the Church always has a place for talented and devoted people. Some of us serve as members of the priesthood but others, like yourself, find different ways that are no less in importance. I have something to tell you and I suggest you brace yourself to receive it."

"I have been asked by the Nuncio of our Holy Mother Church in the United Kingdom to ask you to become a Knight of the Order of Saint Gregory the Great. We have watched you for many years, Liam, and have seen the great works you have performed in the name of Our Lord Jesus Christ. Indeed, such have been your praises that the head of our Order, our Prelate, His Eminence Cardinal Javier Echevarria, no less, recommended that you should receive this high and illustrious title." He paused.

The Pontifical Equestrian Order of St. Gregory the Great was established on 1 September 1831 by Pope Gregory XVI, seven months after his election.

The Order has four classes in civil and military divisions:
- Knight Grand Cross of the First Class
- Knight Grand Cross of the Second Class
- Commander
- Knight

The Order of St Gregory is one of the five pontifical orders of knighthood in the Catholic Church. The order is bestowed on Catholic men and women in recognition of their service to the Church, unusual labours, support of the Holy See, and the good example set in their communities and country.

The Papal Order of Saint Gregory was originally founded by Pope Gregory XVI also on 1 September 1831, in four classes – Knights' Grand Cross (first class), Knights' Grand Cross (second class), Knights' Commander, and Knights. The regulations concerning the grades and uniform were then expanded in a further Bull dated 30 May 1834. As part of the reform of the Papal Orders instituted by Saint Pius X on 7 February 1905, the grades of the Order were modified by the addition of a Star for a higher category of Knights' Commander and the suppression of the second class of Knights' Grand Cross, paralleling the grades of the Ordine Piano and the newly founded Order of Saint Sylvester. Pius X also assigned to the Papal Knights a particular place in Papal processions and in ceremonies of the Church.

Awards of the Order are usually made on the recommendation of Diocesan Bishops or Nuncios for specific services. Unlike membership of the Military Orders (Malta, the Holy Sepulchre, etc), membership of the Order of Saint Gregory does not impose any special obligations. It is thus the preferred award to acknowledge an individual's particular meritorious service to the Church. A Bishop wishing to recommend an individual for this honour will a draw up a suitable letter proposing the candidate's name, with a C.V., and forward it with his recommendation to the Apostolic Nuncio (who may be an Archbishop or Cardinal). The Nuncio may consult with the Bishop regarding the grade – if, perhaps, the grade suggested may be inappropriate – but will then usually forward the recommendation to the Secretariat of State. There the candidate's name is considered carefully and, if approved, a Diploma is drawn up in Latin and this receives the signature and seal of the Cardinal Secretary of State. It is then delivered to the recipient. Usually, Papal awards give rise to a nominal 'tax' charge to cover the expenses concerned – this charge may be paid by the Diocese but is usually reimbursed by the recipient.

The highest rank, that of Grand Cross is an exceptional award – less than eight US citizens have received this honour in the past twenty-two years and those who receive it have usually already been a member of Saint Gregory in one of the lower ranks before being promoted. Knights' Grand Cross wear a more elaborate uniform with more extensive silver braid, a white plumed hat instead of the black plumes common to the lower ranks, while the badge is worn from the broad Riband of the Order on the left hip and the breast star. Knights' Commander wear a less elaborate uniform, with the badge worn suspended from the ribbon of the Order around the neck, while the higher rank (Knights' Commander with Star) also wears the breast star. There have only been twenty-two awards of the senior rank of Commander with Star since 1974 to US citizens. Knights wear a simpler uniform without the braid on the collar and sleeves, with the badge worn from a ribbon suspended on the left breast.

Since 1994, Dames have been admitted in the same grades as men. They do not wear the uniform or sword, their Grand Cross Riband is narrower and the Commander's badge is worn from a bow on the left breast.

And so it was that Liam Burns, who was to become Sir Liam Burns KSt.G. in the autumn, was recommended for this honour by his Bishop, James Herrington, to his Nuncio the Cardinal Basil Wharmsley, Roman Catholic Prelate of the United Kingdom who, in turn, referred the matter to the Prelate of Opus Dei, Cardinal Javier Echevarria who, approving the appointment, added his recommendation and sent it to the Cardinal Secretary of State at the Vatican in Rome. He effectively rubber-stamped the appointment because it was inconceivable that a recommendation coming from the Head of Opus Dei would be questioned, let alone refused.

"I am most honoured. I never expected such an honour," said a visibly shaken Liam Burns to his bishop. He continued, "I really don't think I am worthy, your Excellency. There must be others more deserving."

The Bishop smiled and said gently, "I can assure you, my son, that there are none who approach the degree of devotion to our Order than you do. You must now prepare yourself with renewed fervour and devotion in your fight against Satan and his legions in order to be a pure receptacle for the ceremony of induction which will occur in the second week of October, here at Westminster Cathedral. His Eminence, the Cardinal of Westminster, the leader of all Roman Catholics in the United Kingdom himself, in the presence of our Eminent Prelate shall be the presiding officer." The Bishop rose and taking Liam, who had fallen to his knees in humility, raised him gently saying, "Congratulations, my son. You have done very well."

Liam wept softly.

Immigration and Independence

Liam Burns knelt and prayed to his God with a fervour he had never experienced before. He said, "Lord, you know that I have never asked you for anything before but I must do so now, not for myself but for all of the people in the United Kingdom who revere your holy name. We need your help desperately to stop the Scottish National Party from breaking up this kingdom of yours, a Christian kingdom, a God-fearing kingdom. You will know, Lord, that the opinion polls put Peter Herrings and his party about 75% ahead on the issue of Scottish Independence. We cannot allow this because it will be the start of a slide into idolatry, of false religions of Islam, Judaism, Hinduism and Humanism. Ours is and has always been a country devoted in faith to you alone and although from time to time, I being one of the greatest transgressors, we have made mistakes or drifted away from your goodness and wisdom, nevertheless we have returned to you and you have welcomed us as returning children into your grace. But these idolaters blaspheme your name with their false gods and are not fit to live in your chosen country. I pray, therefore, that you shall raise your mighty hand against the Scottish National Party and dash all hopes of their independent Scotland. I ask this, Lord, in your name alone."

Liam rose and stood for three minutes, deep in contemplation. Upon reading the exit poll statistics earlier that morning, he had temporarily lost all hope that he might secure a 'no' vote in the elections on Scottish Independence, which elections were only one month away. Peter Herrings, the First Minister, had pulled out all the stops to convince the electorate, comprising sixteen and seventeen-year-olds, that his vision of a constitutionally free Scotland was the best for them. He had played the usual 'Braveheart' card ad nauseam repeating the line from the film that 'Scotland regained its freedom' despite the fact that it had not. It had been swallowed up into Great Britain by James VI of Scotland, who became James I of England. The 'Braveheart' warrior was of course William Wallace who failed to create an independent Scotland and, for his treason, met the particularly gruesome death of being hanged, drawn and quartered in the Tower of London. The SNP promised the young kids who were voting for the first time in any election that Scotland would be a country for the young, decided by the young and ruled by the young and the young united into a wave of electoral frenzy, of street parties, marches, internet traffic and fresh-faced support for a half-baked idea.

For the first time in his considerable political career, Liam was staring defeat in the face. He could smell its foul breath in his face, its cold fire intensely on his skin and its wild anarchy overwhelming him.

He needed a miracle, literally.

A year before, Mary Roe was meeting the Greek Finance Minister and Paul Souvereigns at Scholteshof, a very fine restaurant in a small, sleepy village called Stevoort in Belgium.

Being only eighty-five kilometres from Brussels, it was an ideal weekend retreat for Paul and this was a Friday evening.

"Come, Mary, sit down here by the window," said Paul in a mellifluously gracious voice.

Mary sat but, upon looking out of the window onto boring flat scenery, questioned the benefits of such a seat. She smiled sweetly and waited for the attentive waiter to unroll and place the stiffly starched napkin precisely on her lap. The waiter repeated the process for Paul and Nicos Papandreos, the Minister of Finance for the Hellenic Republic of Greece. A waiter then stepped forward and handed a menu to each diner in turn, starting with Mary. She opened it and glanced at the Head Chef's name; it said Roger Souvereyns.

"That's your name isn't it, Paul?" she asked.

"Yes, it is almost so," replied Paul. "In fact, Roger is my uncle, on my father's side."

Just then the Head Waiter approached and bowing slightly, said, "Madame, messieurs, welcome to Scholteshof. I hope you will enjoy the food and wines that we have for you. Do you have a particular dish in mind or may I make some suggestions?"

Paul looked around the table and seeing everyone nod said, "Please feel free to guide us."

Henri Bardet had been the Head Waiter and Sommelier at some of the finest restaurants in Belgium for the previous twenty-five years and smiled graciously at his discerning guests. He asked, "Do you have any allergies or distastes concerning any food products?" None answered and so he continued, "I would suggest the foie gras to start. We serve it at room temperature with a few pieces of toast. Maybe accompanied by a glass of Jurancon? Bon! Now, for the fish course, my recommendation would be the Marinière de Bar à l'huile vierge, which is fresh today, having been caught about four o'clock this morning. You all like sea bass?" Everyone nodded so he continued. "For the wine, I would suggest perhaps a glass of Bergerac Sec."

"I've not heard of that wine, Henri," said Paul.

"Oh, monsieur, it is a much underrated wine, coming as it does from the region next to Bordeaux. It is not well marketed and for years has been, how you say, frowned upon. In fact a famous London wine merchant once said to me that selling Bergerac wine is about as tough as trying to flog a barrel of lard. But I assure you that, if you like sauvignon blanc, you will love this wine, especially the 1988 vintage." He looked around eagerly for approbation and was pleased to receive it.

"Now, for the main course. Do you like lamb?" All nodded. "Then I suggest le carré d'agneau, that is the lamb cutlets with a Parmesan rosemary crust with stuffed onions and zucchini. It is magnifique, so tender, so juicy and our chef cooks it to perfection. It will melt in your mouth." Everyone made noises of appreciation and Henri propelled his enthusiasm forward to the selection of a suitable wine.

"My suggestion to you would be the Gamay Pinot Noir de Touraine, Domaine de la Rochette. We have an excellent 2003 vintage. This wine is dark cerise in colour and is very fruity. It comes from a small vineyard; Francois Leclair only produces forty-six hectares of vines close to the River Cher but his family have been there for three generations. I am sure you will enjoy it. It is far better than any Beaujolais, even a good Fleurie."

And, taking another long pull from her large gin and tonic, it was Mary who said, "I would certainly like to try it if it is that good, thank you Henri."

"Je vous en prie, mademoiselle," said the Head Waiter, taking away the menus.

"He certainly seems to know what he is talking about," said Nico.

"Yes," said Mary, "I'm looking forward to this meal."

The conversation drifted from one topic to another and replacement drinks were ordered. Paul was, as ever, the gracious and sophisticated host and Nico started to flirt with Mary. Mary noticed his amorous advances but was beginning to let go her inhibitions. It could have been the gin or the setting or the company or a combination of everything, she didn't know but she was content, no, excited, to see where the situation would lead. After all she was away from home, her husband of twenty years and the prying eyes of the Scottish Parliament. The starter course arrived, together with the glass of wine, which was smaller than Mary thought it might be. She quite liked it and it certainly went well with the foie gras, which was better than she had tasted before.

"So, I hear you are going for independence in Scotland. When will this be?" asked Nico.

"Oh, the referendum will be held in the summer of 2014 and we expect to have a landslide majority," answered Mary.

Paul cleared his throat and asked, "But won't the English try to prevent this?"

"I expect so, but they won't succeed. The Scottish people want to be free of the English and many of the English are fed up with the Scots. We are targeting the youngsters – the sixteen and seventeen-year-olds who've never voted before, and we're telling them that they can bring us complete freedom as a nation so that we are no longer ruled by any other country. Our slogan is, *Scotland ruled by the Scots for the Scots*. The youngsters really like that idea."

"But, what would you do once you are an independent country?" asked Nico.

"I don't understand you," said Mary.

"Well," continued Nico. "Would you not think of joining the European Union as a sovereign independent nation?"

"Peter, my First Minister and I have spoken a lot about this but we're not sure whether the EU would welcome us. What do you think, Paul?"

"I don't see why not. Europe and Scotland have always had a close bond in the past. There would be a few technicalities to the process of alignment. For example, Scotland would have to join the euro but I think you would find more stability in that currency in the future than with sterling. Certainly, there would also be unfettered access to the European markets for your whisky and other Scottish products. So, I think that, all in all, after alignment, Scotland would be better off. What do you think Nico?"

The fish course came, together with a larger glass of the fine Bergerac Sec that Henri recommended. Everyone agreed that it was a fine wine and Mary found herself getting increasingly merry.

Nico said, "I would agree with you, Paul. I know that we have had a few problems in Greece concerning fiscal alignment but we are supported at every turn by the European Central Bank while we make the necessary changes to our economy. Now, you wouldn't find that kind of support from the Bank of England, would you Mary?"

Mary shook her head; it was distinctly cloudy in there.

Paul put down his cutlery and, wiping his mouth on the napkin, said, "But it's not as simple as that Mary. You know that to make the European Union work, it is necessary to have a strong alignment between nations; adopting a single currency is one idea."

Mary interrupted saying, "I see no objections to Scotland joining the euro but we must keep that a secret between us until after the referendum. You see, people might misunderstand the need for this alignment and, heaven forbid, vote against independence. You do understand Paul, don't you?"

"Of course he does, don't you Paul?" said Nico, placing his hand firmly on Mary's right thigh. She didn't remove it.

"Yes, I do realise the necessity for discretion in this matter but I do not wish to mislead you as to the necessities that must be gone through to achieve alignment. For example, your whisky and haggis products must be aligned to European law for them to be freely marketed throughout Europe." Paul sat back, studying Mary and kicked Nico under the table as he was about to speak.

Mary stopped eating and asked, "What kind of alignment did you mean Paul?"

"Oh, I just meant that they must conform to the law, for example, we have strict labelling laws in Europe. We can't call something by another name; it has to be precise and we need to know where the product comes from. So your whisky would have to state 'made in Scotland' on the label." He paused.

"I don't think that would be a problem. It seems quite sensible in fact," said Mary stroking Nico's hand and slightly raising her skirt so that he could touch the flesh of her thigh.

"And there could be no discrimination between the sexes, absolutely none at all," continued Paul.

"I should hope not," said Mary indignantly. She continued, "I'm all for promoting the benefits of the sexes mixing together harmoniously." She glanced at Nico, who responded by squeezing her thigh.

The main course arrived and all agreed that the lamb was cooked to perfection. A large glass of the red wine arrived and it too was a delicious complement to the meat. They all had a second glass and left empty plates.

Henri returned with the dessert menus. He asked, "Did you enjoy everything up to now?"

They all expressed their delight at the food and wine.

Henri bowed slightly and enquired, "May I suggest you try the fried seasonal fruits with rosemary honey for dessert?" All nodded enthusiastically. "And maybe, I could interest you with a glass of Monbazillac? I have a particularly fine 2003 Vendanges de Brumaire, which is aged in oak barrels for twenty-four months prior to bottling. It gives the wine a superb golden colour."

Everyone expressed their support for the suggestions, albeit in a more than normal carefree manner. Henri bowed again and took away the menus. They all sat contemplating their marvellous dining experience and the warm glow in their bellies.

It was Paul who broke the silence. "So, it would appear, Mary, that we are in agreement concerning alignment and, that being so, I see little objection to the European member states welcoming an independent Scotland into our fold. Welcome!"

The dessert arrived. It was a work of art, comprising a filo pastry shell containing pear, pineapple, papaya, strawberries and mandarin pieces fried in honey, which had been marinated with rosemary and the whole dessert was topped by a sprig of mint. It smelt wonderful and the golden wine was honey-rich, sweet and had a touch of citrus. Everyone applauded Henri when he came back to enquire whether his suggestions had been acceptable.

They retired to an after-dinner room for coffee, petits fours and a twenty-five year old Armagnac. Nico lit a half-corona cigar and all enjoyed the perfume of its smoke. After twenty minutes or so, Paul rose and saying it was time for his bed, asked to be excused. Both Mary and Nico thanked Paul for hosting such a wonderful meal and arranged to meet him for breakfast at nine o'clock the next morning. Nico watched Paul leave and, leaning over to Mary, asked,

"Well, what now?"

Liam Burns could not believe his eyes. A colleague had told him to buy *The Guardian* newspaper, a left-wing rag that he usually wouldn't use for toilet paper let alone read, but he did buy it and there, on the front page, was an article which delighted him. What it said was beyond his wildest dreams. He dropped to his knees and thanked God with all his heart. If ever he had doubted the existence or love of his creator he now knew that God loved him and had answered his prayers.

The referendum to decide Scottish independence was now three weeks away and this newspaper article would dash all hope of an SNP victory. The UK would stay together as Liam wanted and he would be hailed as a victor by the UK Parliament, which had entrusted into Liam's hands the management of a 'no' vote. He had achieved it! What wonders would political life now have in store for him, a leading government minister who, in a few months, would be inducted into the Equestrian Order of St Gregory the Great. He fell to his knees and praised and thanked God for His generosity and love.

The article, written by Bill Fillingrue-Smythe, the Editor-in-Chief of *The Guardian* newspaper was entitled **'*Europe Bans the Scottish Kilt*'**. It continued:

'Following a meeting last year in Belgium with Scotland's Deputy First Minister, the EU Commissioner for Justice, Paul Souvereyns, wishes to make it clear that, if Scotland becomes independent following its referendum next month, then it will have to conform to strict rules of alignment if it wishes to become a member of the European Union and, for the first three years, that membership will be as a third nation. This means that Scotland will not enjoy the benefits and opt outs which were negotiated by the United Kingdom but, instead will be subject to the full obligations and expenses of a normal member state. Moreover, for that three-year probationary period it will be unable to vote at any Treaty debate.

Paul Souvereyns also points out that he discussed the various points of alignment with Mary Roe, the Deputy First Minister at their meeting in Belgium and she said that she foresaw no problems for Scotland. He said that, having read the statements forthcoming from the SNP ahead of the referendum, he wishes to clarify a number of points so that the Scottish people will be under no illusions as to their obligations should they wish to join the European Union. He summarised the points as follows:

1.   Scotland would be compelled to join the euro. This would necessitate Scots changing their money into sterling should they wish to visit England or Wales.

2.   The Scots would not be subject to the rules of the Bank of England. The European Central Bank would do all of the financial administration for the Scottish Parliament.

3.   Due to the stance taken by the United Kingdom in the past, strict border controls would be enforced between

Scotland and the rest of the (now) UK. This would involve the issue of Scottish passports which would need to comply with EU biometrics regulations.

4. *Kilts would be outlawed. They are discriminatory as only men are allowed to wear them; women are prohibited except where they are part of a pipe band.*

5. *Likewise and for the same reasons, sporrans would be banned.*

6. *Haggis could no longer be sold under that name because of strict EU labelling laws. Instead the product would be renamed, 'Emulsified meat and offal bag', which the Commissioner feels is a more accurate description of the product.*

7. *Scottish whisky would be banned because its alcohol content is too high. The Commissioner explained that whereas Scotch whisky is 40% by volume, the average European equivalent is only 28% by volume. He said, "The Scottish people will just have to add water to their product if they wish to sell it in Europe." Asked why, he said, "It is the law and besides there are too many people in Scotland getting drunk and falling about in the streets. Our European police force, when it is formed in about three years time, will not allow this kind of behaviour in any member state and, you must remember, we have many prisons with spare capacity in the European Union; Romania and Bulgaria are two examples."*

8. *Apparently, anyone who commits a crime in one EU country, could find himself serving time in a prison in a foreign country. When asked about this, the Commissioner said, "This is true. If you commit a crime in, say, Scotland, then you may well find that you will be sent to a prison in Romania or Italy or somewhere else. It depends upon spare*

capacity in all of the prisons in Europe. We are introducing a full computer system which will keep track of the availability of prison space throughout the EU. It will be more efficient and cost-effective than the way we do things now."

> **9.** *Scotland would lose control over its waters which would continue to be a European resource. Because Scotland would be a third nation for three years on entering the EU, it would have no fishing quota allocated to it for that period. When questioned about this, the Commissioner said, " I see no problem. The Scots and the French have always been good friends and I am sure that the French would be very willing to sell fish to the Scottish people. They would not go without."'*

The article continued: *'So, now you know what Scottish Independence will mean to you. Don't say The Guardian didn't warn you. Bill Fillingrue-Smythe, Editor-in-Chief.'*

Peter Herrings sat in the Cabinet Office in Bute House, his head in his hands, knowing that all he'd worked for over the last thirty years was in tatters. The newspaper on the table in front of him said it all.

"But I didn't say that!" exclaimed Mary Roe. "And he didn't tell me all this would happen. Do you think I would have agreed if I'd known, Peter? You must believe me!"

"Leave me alone, please, Mary," groaned Scotland's First Minister and, waiving her away, Mary Roe left the office in tears.

Three weeks later, the referendum result was presented by the Presiding Officer of the City of Edinburgh. He said:

"The results of the referendum as to whether Scotland should become independent of the United Kingdom are as follows:

1. Those in favour 31%
2. Those against 64%
3. Don't knows 5%

I declare that the motion is defeated."

The Chamber of the House of Commons erupted in cheering and a jubilation that had never been seen before; it was akin to rude foolings.

In contrast, Peter Herrings sat alone, his head in his hands in the Cabinet Office in Bute House, Edinburgh. He had been there motionless for the past three hours. The phone rang. He answered it.

"Peter? Peter Herrings?" the voice asked.

"Yes, who's this?"

"It is Paul, Paul Souvereyns from the Commission."

"Oh aye. What do you want? Do you want to gloat more? You really stuck the boot in, didn't you? Destroyed thirty years of my hard political work and you did it in one week. Ock, I don't know why I'm talking to you. It's the wrong time."

"But wait. Don't hang up Peter. I want to talk to you."

"Oh aye, what about?"

"Peter, you do not know how much you have impressed people here at the Commission. You very nearly won and brought a whole sovereign nation into our Community. That is very impressive, not even Tony Blair could do that. Well, to cut to the quick, I think that is how you say it."

"Chase. Cut to the chase, you mean," was the reply.

"Yes, to the chase. The European Union wants you to be a Commissioner, in fact the Commissioner for emerging nations. You would have offices here in Brussels, together with four regional offices, probably in former palaces or hunting lodges throughout Europe. You would be travelling extensively and therefore you would need your own private jet and Bentley, unless of course you prefer a Rolls Royce or maybe a nice sports car or two. Your salary of course would be limited to about four hundred thousand euros but with the indirect benefits derived from advising private organisations, I would estimate your yearly income to be in the region of two and a half million euros, tax free. We could also accommodate most generously, your deputy Mary, should you wish. What do you say?"

Peter straightened up and said immediately, "I accept."

The voice on the telephone asked, "And will you be bringing Mary with you?"

The curt reply was, "I will be alone. I've finished with women."

Peter Herrings replaced the phone and rising, went to look out of the window. The sun, though still shining brightly, had lost some of its radiance; the leaves were falling and there seemed to be a slight chill in the air. He turned and looking around thought:

"Yes, it's time to go."

Immigration and Flexibility

"Come in, James and sit down next to me," said the Prime Minister beckoning the Immigration Minister to a comfortable leather chair on the other side of the ornate fireplace. James sat.

"I'm most impressed with you," continued the Prime Minister, smiling and regarding him with shrewd unsmiling eyes.

"I'm very pleased to have been given an opportunity to serve your Government, Prime Minister."

"Yes quite," was the answer. "You seem to have become a Mr Fix-it to many of our most difficult problems. In fact, you have solved more deep-rooted administrative problems than any other person I know. Previous administrations would, I feel, have given their right arms to have you on side." He paused. James beamed. The PM continued, "I've got you earmarked for one of the great offices of state. Now, you can't have Chancellor because I've got that allocated to Jeremy and I'm minded to leave Cecil in charge of the Foreign Office. However, there's always the Home Office and I think that you'd do rather well there, judging by your successes in that area. What do you think, potential Home Secretary?" He sat back, smiling and watching James Greene.

James was completely taken aback but tried his best not to show it. He said, "It would be an honour to serve you in whatever capacity you would think me fit."

"Good. Good," said the Prime Minister. "I think you would make a fine Home Secretary. Now, we've got a bit of a political problem and I think you can solve it, seeing as it falls within your area of expertise." James sat up attentively. The Prime Minister continued, "Yes. As you know, next year, Romania and Bulgaria become full members of the European Union. This means that their illiterate citizens will have a right to come to the UK, claim our benefits, commit their crimes, give venereal disease to our women and we won't be able to remove them." He paused.

"Yes it is a problem," said James Greene.

"Well, I want you to solve it, James. You're a capable lad. I don't want them here."

"I'll try Prime Minister but it is very difficult, you know."

"Yes, but you are more capable than the rest and I'm sure your life will be much easier when you become Home Secretary. Let us say that this small test is designed to show all of your political opponents how really ruthless you can be when pushed. What do you say, James?"

James Greene did not hesitate but said immediately, "I accept, Prime Minister." He knew that the doors of political opportunities open seldomly and he was determined to be there standing alone when those doors opened. The Prime Minister stood up and shook James's hand to signify that the meeting was over.

On his way back to his office in Lunar House, Croydon, James wracked his brain for a way in which he could solve this problem; he could think of none. The Romanians and Bulgarians, as full members of the EU had a perfect right to travel to any other EU member state. It was a right enshrined in the very heart of the Treaty of Rome, namely Article 30. No law or court in the EU could stop it happening for any normal reason, except perhaps on health grounds under an Article 36 Derogation. He didn't think such a legal argument might apply here because, although the Romanians and Bulgarians had many undesirable qualities, he didn't think they constituted a health hazard to other European citizens. He didn't know what to do and so he went home to his semi-detached house in Coulsdon.

He switched on the television next morning as he was making coffee and he saw that the Germans were having a go at the French because French imports of beef were found to contain horse meat. Apparently, Germany was about to ban French meat imports per se. He decided to keep an eye on this situation even though it had nothing to do with him. It certainly had to do with the Health Secretary and the Secretary of State for Environment, Food and Rural Affairs and he thought that both of his government colleagues needed the exercise of a challenging political issue.

On arrival at his office in Croydon, he switched on the television and was surprised to note that Belgium and the UK had joined in the argument with France. Germany had decided in principle to ban French meat products, a view supported by the Belgium. Holland, Austria, Spain, Portugal and Italy were on the point of deciding likewise. The British were sitting on the fence. James picked up the phone.

"Hello David, it's James. You've got a bit of a problem I see."

David Baillie, the Secretary of State for Health said, "Don't tell me about it James. I've got everyone demanding that I ban meat imports from France because of this wretched horse meat scandal. I've got the French on the other phone threatening to ban all of our meat exports if we ban their meat and, quite frankly, I don't know what to do for the best."

"What about Jason?" asked James. "Isn't he handling this? Why are you involved?"

"Jason Roberts?" answered David. He continued, "Our whiz kid of Environment, Food and Rural Affairs? He's about as much use as a dose of diarrhoea to a man with a chronic cough! He tried to wash his hands of the whole affair; says it is a health problem, not a food supply-chain issue. You know he's a little shit, James."

"What are you going to do, David?"

"Haven't a clue. Haven't a clue James."

James Greene thought for a minute and then said slowly, "I've got an idea. Leave it with me for a couple of weeks. No promises, David."

"You're a brick," said the Health Secretary and they hung up.

"Justice Commissioner's office. How can I help you?" asked a delicately modulated female voice.

"Paul Souveryns, please. James Greene UK Immigration Minister."

A few minutes later a voice said, "James! How good to hear from you. How's everything?"

"Good Paul. Tell me something; are you interested in controlling a bit more of Europe's justice systems?"

"Of course I am, James. Do you want me to take over your job? Not up to it, eh?"

"Calm down, Paul. I want to know something. How far can you bend Article 30 of the Treaty of Rome?"

"Very little, James. I mean, it's at the heart of the European Union; it is our foundation. I mean, on rare occasions we can modify it a little on, say, health grounds by means of an Article

36 Derogation but that would happen rarely and the evidence would have to be overwhelming."

"Yes, I understand, but could it be done to prevent a larger violation of Article 30?"

"I don't know what you mean James. Please explain."

Paul, have you heard from the Germans and Belgians about their plan to ban all French meat imports?"

"Yes, I have."

"Can it be done, Paul?"

"No, not under EU law. Certainly not."

"Well, what would happen if the Germans said that they were going to do it anyway?" asked James.

Paul immediately responded, "But they couldn't do it. It is against the law."

"But what would happen if they said that they didn't care about the law, that they were going to ban the imports regardless?" asked James.

"We would have to take steps against them. It is obvious," said Paul.

"Like fining them?" asked James.

"Yes, at least," said Paul.

"Well, what would you do if Germany refused to pay the fine and threatened to withdraw from the European Union?"

"But that's impossible, James. That would bankrupt the Union," said Paul.

James said quietly and slowly, "I agree and that's the problem you've got. I think you'll find that Belgium, Austria, Spain, Portugal and Italy will follow suit."

"Impossible!" exclaimed Paul. "What about the UK?"

"I think they'd also leave. You know we are not that committed to membership of the EU." He paused.

"Yes, I had a long conversation with your Prime Minister on this subject not long ago," said Paul.

"Well then, Paul, you know the likely outcome."

"Is there no way out of this, James? Can you help?"

"Me, Paul? I can't help, but I know someone who can."

"Who James? Tell me, who?"

"Well, Paul, I think the best people to help here are the ones who caused the problem in the first place." He paused and said, "The French. I'll have a word with them to see if there is a way around this problem. Can I rely on your support, Paul?"

"You will certainly have more than my support if you can solve this issue, James. Have you ever considered being a Commissioner yourself?"

James laughed and said, "Thanks, Paul, but one problem at a time." He put down the phone and then dialled the Foreign and Commonwealth Office.

Sir Donald Evans, Her Britannic Majesty's Ambassador to Europe sat opposite his French counterpart, His Excellency M. Maurice Fournier, the French Ambassador in the Élysée Palace, situated at 55 Rue du Faubourg Saint-Honoré, at its intersection with Avenue de Marigny. They were seated in the magnificent Salon Dore (the Golden Room) on the first floor. As they sipped a particularly elegant XO champagne cognac, the French Ambassador turned and asked:

"So, Donald, how can I help the English?"

Sir Donald Evans smiled gently and said, "Maurice, I think it is you who needs England's support."

"In what way does France need the English? I've never known this before and although I doubt what you say, I shall listen. It may prove to be, amusant, ne c'est pas?"

Sir Donald waited and let the insult flow over him. He leaned back and asked, "Selling much meat, Maurice?"

The French Ambassador's face darkened like thunder and he quickly said, "We are doing alright. Sales are slightly down this month but that is quite understandable under the circumstances."

Sir Donald said, "Your country's sales of meat products have been devastated by this horse meat scandal and you know it. There are six countries about to ban all imports of meat products from France and several more may join them. Moreover, you needn't look to the Commission to help you because they will back Germany, which has threatened to leave the EU. There's no way the Commission will allow that for obvious financial reasons. So, it seems you're on your own, Maurice." Sir Donald took another sip of his cognac and savoured its elegant taste.

"But, I do not know what is all the fuss about," said Maurice Fournier. "This is good meat. OK, so it contains a little horse or donkey in it. We, in France, eat these things. It does not harm anyone."

"OK," said Sir Donald, "then you shouldn't have any trouble convincing the Germans and the rest of the EU countries, including the United Kingdom, which you seem to like to insult." And rising, Sir Donald said, "But if that's what you want, Maurice, I wish you luck."

The French Ambassador rose and, taking Sir Donald gently by the arm, said, "Donald, let us not be too hasty in this matter. Surely, you have time for another cognac? It's particularly good, ne c'est pas?" The two Ambassadors sat down and their glasses were replenished. "What is it that you would suggest, Sir Donald," asked Maurice.

"Well Maurice, I was thinking that the United Kingdom and the Republic of France have been friends and allies for many centuries. It is true that, on a few occasions, we have not always agreed with each other, but those minor issues should not prevent either of us from offering help to the other."

"I absolutely agree, Sir Donald. What do you propose?"

Sir Donald felt that a deal was imminent and went in for the kill. "I propose," he said, "that the UK supports France in resisting the ban on French meat products." He sat back.

"But why would you do this? What is in it for the United Kingdom?" asked an astonished French Ambassador.

"I don't suppose there would be any reciprocal obligation, Maurice. It is just one ally helping another at an hour of need and it would be a very sad world if we could not continue our mutual co-operation, don't you think?"

"Absolutely," said a delighted Maurice Fournier.

Sir Donald continued, "I think our Prime Minister could convince the German Chancellor to go along with us. There would be a political price to pay but I'm sure your Government would not object as long as it did not impact upon the Common Agricultural Policy?" Sir Donald raised his eyebrows and was greeted with a smile and a nod from his opponent. He took another sip from his glass and paused.

Maurice Fournier put down his glass and asked, "And you would do all of this for France, for free?"

"Absolutely" smiled Sir Donald and said, "Oh, by the way, can we change the subject, Maurice? Please tell me how the French got into this mess. Does French beef normally contain horse meat?"

The French Ambassador said warily, "You know, Sir Donald, that we French do eat horse meat. We also eat beef. But we keep both food products separate from each other. Now, you must understand that this latest crisis is not of our making. We acted in good faith but we have been criminally misled."

Sir Donald quickly interjected, "But in what way, Maurice?" He knew exactly how but wanted the Frenchman to admit it.

"We had a rare opportunity to buy beef at a very low price from Romania and Bulgaria. Mon Dieu! The prices of European beef are far too expensive. So, as you can imagine, we jumped at the opportunity to buy Romanian beef at a tenth of the cost of our French beef. The quality seemed good and there was a plentiful supply of it and everything seemed fine. Our prices were very competitive and we soon achieved a dominant status throughout Europe for these products. We have been supplying this type of meat for the last eight years and nobody complained until the bloody Germans, pardon my French, did their stupid tests and found horse meat in their burgers. And now we have this problem."

Sir Donald asked, "But why would the Romanians and Bulgarians doctor their beef exports? They must have known that they would get caught eventually."

"They did not care," said the French Ambassador. "The mafia over there runs this supply chain. They also have links with the mafia in Bulgaria. They control all of the slaughterhouses in those countries and the transport, so they can buy a donkey or horse carcass for less than a euro and then sell us a kilo of processed meat for three euros. That is incredibly cheap and we buy millions of kilos a year. So they make a great deal of money criminally, but what can we do, Donald?"

"Maurice, I think I can help you if you will help me."

"Anything within my power, Donald."

They talked intently and quietly for the next two hours and then, smilingly, went into the dining room to enjoy a sumptuous meal.

The headlines in *The Guardian* newspaper the following week stated: **'France opposes the entry of Romania and Bulgaria into the European Union.'**

It continued:

'In an exclusive interview with The Guardian, the French Ambassador to the EU, His Excellency M. Maurice Fournier said that his government had decided to oppose Romania's and Bulgaria's admission into the EU because there were so many criminal elements in those countries where the mafia operates without any state control, that he felt that giving them access to a free market would result in widespread corruption throughout every member state of the EU.

Britain was asked for its view and James Greene, our Immigration Minister, said that HM's Government felt deeply for the view expressed by the French. He said that the UK had long cast doubts on the suitability of those two countries having full membership rights. He also said that the UK and France were not alone in this view. Germany, Austria, Belgium, Spain, Portugal and Italy had also expressed strong views in the same way.'

We asked the Commission for its views and Paul Souveryns said: *'It is the Commission's view that, taking everything into account and taking advice from leading representatives of the member states, that it is too soon for Romania and Bulgaria to become full members of the European Union. He suggested that both countries should attend to their internal matters and apply for membership perhaps in fifteen years' time.'*

The article was signed Bill Fillingrue-Smythe, Editor-in-Chief.

The phone rang and James Greene answered it.

"Hello James. Chief Whip here. The PM wants to see you this afternoon at Number 10. Two thirty. Don't be late."

The Prime Minister rose when he heard the knock on the door. "James Greene and the Chief Whip, Prime Minister."

"Show them in please." They entered; the Chief Whip first, who stood aside to reveal an embarrassed Immigration Minister. "James, James, come in," said the Prime Minister, striding across the carpet with his right hand outstretched. They shook hands and the PM asked, "How are you, dear boy?" He led James to a comfortable chair and offered him a drink.

"You pulled it off, didn't you?" he said, smiling paternally at James. He continued, "Don't have to put up with a torrent of illiterate foreigners invading us from Romania and Bulgaria next year and stealing our benefits, committing their crimes and giving our women venereal disease. I can't wait to see the Leader of the Opposition's face when I tell him about this tomorrow in the House. He'll be livid with envy and it's all down to you, my boy."

James beamed a large smile and humbly said, "It was nothing, Prime Minister."

"Yes it was!" boomed the Prime Minister, "and you will remember what I said about rewarding you if you were successful? Well I've asked the Chief Whip to attend this meeting so that he can confirm that I am now appointing you my Home Secretary, effective as of today. What do you think of that?"

James was overwhelmed and could only mutter, "Thank you, Prime Minister. I shall do my best."

When the meeting was over, James walked along Whitehall, reached into his coat pocket for his mobile phone, dialled a number and said, "Yo wanker! Big nosebag today." He paused and then said:

"You're speaking to the new Home Secretary."

165

The morning's *Guardian* said: **'Immigration Minister is new Home Secretary'**.

It continued: *'The Guardian has just learned that James Greene, our Immigration Minister, was appointed Home Secretary yesterday by the Prime Minister. It is no secret that this newspaper has not always seen eye to eye with Mr Greene but it hopes that everyone can put the past behind them and work happily together in the future. The Guardian says well done James, our new Home Secretary.'*

It was signed Bill Fillingrue-Smythe, Editor-in-Chief.

Immigration and Gratitude

Bill Fillingrue-Smythe sat motionless staring at the letter that he had just opened. It was neatly-typed in Arial type twelve point on 120-gsm Conqueror paper with the crest of HM The Queen, squarely in the middle at the top of the letter which read:

'Her Majesty has the greatest pleasure in inviting William Fillingrue-Smythe to become a Knight (second class) of the Most Noble Order of the Bath for services to journalism.'

He simply said, "Shit!" and read it again ... and again ... and again. The phone rang and he answered it, "Bill Fillingrue-Smythe?"

James Greene said, "Have you got it yet, Bill?"

"What? What? You mean the letter?"

"Yes, have you got it yet?"

"Just looking at it now. Can't believe it. It's real. It's here. I'm one of them."

"Congratulations, Sir William," said James Greene. He continued, "I promised you the K."

"Yes, I know you did, but I didn't believe you. I thought you'd double-crossed me, James. You can't blame me can you after what happened before?"

James Greene said, "Bill, that was your fault for blabbing about it before you got your official letter. I had a hell of a job turning it around but look, I don't want to start the blame game. You've got it and that's all that matters, Bill. Congratulations."

Bill replied, "Thanks, James. You're a brick. Listen, if there's anything you want, anything at all, you let me know. Anything, you hear me?"

"Thanks, Bill, but I don't need anything. After all, if you can't help a friend now and again, well what can you do? Anyway I just wanted to ring and congratulate you. Bye Bill." They hung up and James went to his antique Georgian desk and, pouring himself a large malt whisky, thought, *yes, I will have a very large one, Bill, and also in the future and at your considerable expense.*

Kate Jones and Liam Burns were having dinner at the Regency Hotel in High Holborn in London. It was only fifteen minutes away from the Houses of Parliament where they both worked. Liam was busily explaining what his Auxiliary Bishop had said to him. He explained that admission to the Equestrian Order of St Gregory the Great was a great honour and only rarely conferred on a member of the Roman Catholic Church. He failed to notice Kate's look of glowing admiration.

"This calls for a celebration," she said. "Let's have a bottle of white wine."

"But I don't drink alcohol," he said, "and nor should you."

"Why?" she asked.

"Because it is against the rules and ordinances of our Order."

"Poppycock!" she said and continued, "Did not Our Lord change water into wine at the Marriage Feast of Canaan?"

"Well, yes," agreed Liam hesitantly.

"So why is wine evil if our Blessed Lord approved of it?"

Liam had no answer, so Kate continued, "So let's try a bottle and if we don't like it, we'll have something else." She collared a passing waiter and ordered a bottle of Chardonnay Reserve from a small Israeli vineyard near the border with Jordan. She said, "You know, Liam, Our Lord could have been drinking this over two thousand years ago in the Holy Land." The waiter brought a wine cooler, presented the bottle to Liam, who deferred to Kate, and then poured a little into Kate's glass to taste. Kate approved it saying that it was wonderful and Liam wondered how she knew. The waiter then filled Kate's and Liam's glasses and Liam lifted the glass to his nose, tentatively smelling the amber coloured liquid. It smelled like honey and green grass to him so he placed a little in his mouth. It tasted of golden, honeyed, fruity nectar, like the most glorious summer's day in the Cotswolds. He took a bigger drink and beaming at Kate, said, "It's very good, isn't it?"

Kate looked longingly at Liam and replied, "Well you don't think that Our Lord would be a party to anything sordid, do you?"

They enjoyed a wonderful meal, washed down by two bottles of the same wine so that Liam, who had never experienced the effects of alcohol before, was unexpectedly transported to some kind of seventh heaven, which he enjoyed immensely.

"What are your plans for this evening, Liam?" she asked. "You obviously can't go back to Netherhall House like that. They'll know you've been drinking."

"What do you suggest?" he asked.

"Why don't we stay here? You can always blame your absence on an all-night sitting." It made sense. He nodded.

Kate booked a room with a double bed for both of them. Liam didn't notice in his inebriated state. Kate hoped that Liam had not had so much as to invoke a physical state commonly called 'brewer's droop'. She decided to take control of the situation and, adopting her most matronly voice, said,

"Come on Liam. Let me put you to bed." He readily agreed, being halfway between earthly rapture and heavenly bliss. He thought he could even hear angels singing. She slipped in beside him, her naked body curling around his. He was barely aware of his manhood rising like a stalk in a Jack and the Beanstalk pantomime. It felt quite good, especially when Kate waggled it. He'd never felt this sensation. She rolled him onto his back and straddled him. His first thought about being pushed into her was that it felt hot, very hot. It wasn't particularly pleasant, just hot; it was a strange sensation. And then the longing commenced like a nagging urge and he started to push, slowly at first and then with increasing momentum. She gasped and Liam rolled her onto her back and pinned her there thrusting harder and faster into her.

Like most women, Kate thought: *He's filled with love for me.*

Like most men, Liam thought: *How can I ram the end of my dick out of the top of her head?*

They met in the same Chinese restaurant in Paddington Street exactly one week later.

Yang Chen said to Lai Qianxian as they ate, "I'm very grateful you could come, Lai."

"I didn't have much choice did I? How's my family, Yang?"

"In perfect health. In fact they're doing very well indeed. They've just moved into a much bigger house with all the amenities, just on the outskirts of the city, in a particularly nice suburb."

"But they couldn't afford anything like that; they don't earn enough."

Yang leaned forward, and pouring more sake into Lai's glass said, "Who said anything about money? Consider it a little gift from our Government as a thank you for your co-operation.

We don't always take you know. We're just a big family at the end of the day, a family that knows how to look after each other."

He sat back and his eyes hardened. "I want your help, Lai," he said.

"What do you want me to do?"

"Not much," Yang replied. "I want you to introduce me to someone you know, someone who works for the Cabinet Office, a chap called Wah Lam."

"Wah? I hardly know him. I know we sit occasionally on the same Security Committee but apart from that, I hardly know him."

"Then get to know him better and tell him I want to meet him here at our weekly meetings."

"What about?"

"That doesn't concern you, just get him here," was Yang's reply.

A week later, Lai and Yang met in the same restaurant. "Well?" asked Yang. "What did he say?"

Lai paused for a moment and decided to tell it exactly as it was. "He said he's not going to meet you. He said that he doesn't like the sound of it and if there's anything more, he'll report you. I've done my best Yang. What more can I do?"

Yang thought for a moment and, placing a hand on Lai's arm, gently said, "You've done well, Lai. Don't worry. I'll deal with this. Next week, OK?"

The following week they met and Yang said, "Has your friend changed his mind, Lai?" Lai shook his head and Yang pushed a small rectangular box across the table saying, "Could you please give this to Wah? Tell him it contains his father's spectacles; he won't be needing them any more seeing as we removed his eyes a few days ago. There's also a cassette tape from his mother explaining the events, her promised fate and that of his four sisters. Tell him that his nine-year-old sister will make a particularly popular prostitute in the barracks of one of the regiments of the People's Republic of China. Lai, tell him I want him here, next week at the latest or I'll do what I say and then start on his aunts and uncles, nephews and nieces ... and then I'll start on his wife, his children and him. Tell him Lai."

Next week, they all met in the same restaurant and Yang Chen introduced himself to the other two. He observed that where Lai was tall and thin, Wah was short, fat and wore thick spectacles. He dispensed with the formalities and cut to the chase. "Wah, I know you work for the Cabinet Office and I want information, a lot of information. I want to know all the business that concerns national security, including infrastructure backup, banking contingencies and all commercial procurement projects, especially where the UK is bidding for contracts in Africa, the Middle East and the Far East."

"But I can't give you that! It's top secret. It's private. Only the Cabinet Ministers know that." His eyes grew bigger, like two dark saucers brimming with tears.

Yang leaned forward and hissed, "What do you take me for? A total idiot? I know that Cabinet meetings are secret and we cannot know their discussions as they are presented on a need-to-know basis to each Minister. However, when a Minister needs to implement a Cabinet decision, then his officials need to produce all manner of documents; briefing papers, project mandates, etcetera. It is these documents I want, especially Ministry of Defence and Trade and Industry papers. If you can get me anything interesting like NATO communications or Echelon exchanges, I would be most grateful and Lai here will tell you how grateful I can be."

"But I can't get you MOD documents. They're top secret and like all top secret documents they are only ever communicated over dedicated telephone lines with a Northrop decoder at each end."

Yang interjected, "I know about Northrop decoders. Are they still unlinked or are they coded in pairs?"

"No, they are completely independent of each other; they need to be, for how could an encryptor from, say the Special Branch in the Wiltshire Constabulary, pair with an encryptor, say in the Security Service at Thames House otherwise?"

"Good, that's what I thought. Right I want a Northrop encryptor, Wah. There must be some lying around, maybe waiting for repair or something. Get it for me and do it quickly before I stop being so generous with your family's future."

"But it won't work without a dedicated line," said Wah quickly.

"I can get a dedicated line from British Telecom any time I want. Do you think that you two are the only Chinese nationals working for me? Get it for me, oh, and I want to know from you Wah, about the use of the black and red channels. Is there a daily sequence or what?"

"No," said Wah. "You choose either one and the recipient decoder adjusts itself to the same channel automatically."

"OK," said Yang. "Now, what about Echelon? How do I get a stream of relevant information from that system?"

"It's not easy, you know. We don't run this facility. It's the FBI who are in control. They barely trust us since the Bosnian/Serbian conflict when we were passing intelligence to the French and they were passing it straight on to the Serbs. As a result, we would mount an ambush for the Serbs and they would be hundreds of miles away burning another Bosnian village."

"I don't accept this," said Yang. "The intercepts of phrases containing code words must land on someone's desk. I want a telecommunications divert from those duty intelligence officers' desks to my secure line here at the Embassy. I know this can be done Wah and I know you can do it because you and your team handle all of this secure infrastructure. So get to it and give me a result!"

Echelon is a worldwide communications monitoring system. The UK's satellite hub for the system is situated at RAF Menwith Hill in North Yorkshire; it is the biggest communications station in Europe. The job of Echelon is to listen in to every telephone call, land based or mobile, every email and every satellite communication for phrases or words of interest. For example, if you were to say, 'Muslim extremist' or a similar phrase, then your entire conversation would arrive on the desk of one of many of the duty intelligence analysts who would decide whether or not you constitute a threat to national or international security. The first you would know about it would be a heavily armed police squad breaking down the door of your house in Bradford or Leeds. The Cray supercomputers, which power Echelon, can work at several hundred million instructions per second. Surprisingly, the supercomputer is very small, say the size of a small refrigerator, but the most amazing feature of it is its cooling fluid, which runs down one side of the computer room, like a waterfall. It is a joy to behold.

Before they left Yang said, "Wah, I want you to put a key word into Echelon."

"What word?" asked Wah.

Yang simply said, "Chinese" and left the restaurant.

Immigration and Revenge

Sid Vickery and Jonathan Findus settled themselves into the false cupboard in Room 422 of the Regency Hotel in High Holborn. The hotel was a mere fifteen minutes by taxi from Parliament Square and maybe that was why Liam Burns and Kate Jones chose it for their twice weekly romantic liaisons. On the face of it, there was nothing wrong because neither of them was married, but Bill Fillingrue-Smythe had sent Sid and Jonathan, two of his best undercover reporters, to the hotel to film the couple because he knew that Liam and Kate were Opus Dei numeraries and, as such, had taken a solemn vow of celibacy. Bill wanted to destroy Liam's political career in a spectacular front page article, a scoop for that left-wing rag, *The Guardian*. He hated Liam because he had nearly destroyed the career of Bill's friend, John Prendergast, a Deputy Secretary with the Home Office. Moreover Bill suspected that Liam had been behind the embarrassing fiasco when James Greene had promised Bill a Knighthood, the first time around and, despite the fact that he had eventually received his K, Bill was not one to forgive treachery of any kind.

The happy couple, united in the joys of the flesh, praised each other and praised God in their mutual passion. At least, that's what Jonathan understood on hearing Kate gasp, "Oh my God! Oh my God!" But, then again, Jonathan was not particularly religious. In fact, he only ever went to church for the births, deaths and marriages of members of his West Country extended family, an organised crime syndicate. That was not to say that he was stupid: far from it. He was resourceful, shrewd, credible and well skilled in the disciplines of the police. He had enjoyed an illustrious career as a Detective Sergeant with the Croydon Constabulary for twenty-five years and had retired on a full pension.

Sid was altogether a different type of person. He, too, had been a Detective Sergeant with the same force, had served for twenty-five years and had also retired on a full police pension, the same as Jonathan. But there the similarities ended. Where Jonathan was resourceful, Sid delegated all tasks to his trusted employees and associates. Where Jonathan was shrewd, Sid knew when to act and when to leave things alone. Where Jonathan was credible, Sid was faceless: the power behind the throne. Where Jonathan was well skilled in the disciplines of the police, Sid was well skilled in the disciplines of many European police forces and some of the UK's security services. Sid was the planner and Jonathan managed the muscle because, on many occasions, they were called in to get evidence, either photographic or witness statements, in situations involving organised criminal gangs. *The Guardian* newspaper did not care how Sid and Jonathan got the evidence, so long as it was accurate and factual; the consequences didn't matter. There was one incident, when the newspaper was tracking a particularly nasty group of Romanians operating a financial scam involving ATM machines, when Sid found himself separated from Jonathan and facing a particularly ugly foreigner who was armed with a two foot length of lead piping. The Romanian threatened to break both of Sid's legs for his interference in their business. No-one knows exactly what happened after that because Sid would not say, but the Romanian was found in an alley in Northallerton with the lead pipe rammed down his throat – literally. As regards Jonathan, well he seemed to favour the use of small weapons and many a time there would be a police report concerning a shooting of minor hoodlums or immigrants; Jonathan did not like foreigners.

That is not to say that professional life was without major incidents. Many times Sid and Jonathan had been interviewed under caution by the police but there was never a charge or a conviction, mainly because Sid and Jonathan could prove that they were somewhere else at the time, an alibi fully corroborated by Sir William Fillingrue-Smythe, their boss, and let's face it, who in the police would go up against the Editor-in-Chief of a leading UK daily and a Knight of the realm to boot? Bill felt that he could send this pair to do any job, large or small, and he knew he would always get a good result and on time. And so it was that Sid and Jonathan found themselves in the false cupboard of the wardrobe of Room 422, filming Liam and Kate bonking the hell (no pun intended) out of each other. They seemed to like it a lot, thought Jonathan who, himself, was no believer in paucity or half measures when it came to his turn. They filmed on and on, with Kate on top of Liam; with Liam behind Kate; they got a very good sequence of Kate sucking Liam's manhood and of the final dash to the mutual exchange of bodily fluids and the experience of the narrow divide between life and death. They even filmed the couple in their inaugural attempts at anal sex but they noted that Kate asked Liam to stop as she felt that that technique was just a pain in the bum. Sid and Jonathan laughed, although very quietly. Nor was it all work; they had brought their sandwiches with them and a thermos flask of coffee. They enjoyed these while monitoring the progress the couple were making towards 'burying the sausage' as Liam had put it and, they had to confess, that he had a very big sausage to bury. In fact, it was not far off being a saveloy. Eventually, after three sessions this time, the couple finished, expressed their everlasting love, dressed and left the room, presumably intent on returning to Parliament and guiding the nation in the paths of truth and righteousness.

James Greene stared in horror at the front page of *The Guardian* newspaper. It said: '*Birmingham Primary Hospital Trust can confirm the deaths of two Indian visitors due to their inability to pay for life-saving treatment. A senior executive, John Craig, said, "We deeply regret the deaths of Mr and Mrs Patel but we were helpless to save them. We couldn't give them any care at all. You see, we are operating under the direct orders of the Health Secretary and, in the case of foreign visitors to the UK, the Minister for Immigration, James Greene, has given strict orders that unless visitors to the UK can pay for healthcare, no hospital trust in England or Wales may treat them. In the old days, we would have had no problem in helping these two unfortunate people and our doctors say that they could have saved Mr and Mrs Patel. It's so very, very sad and this tragic incident could have been avoided."*' We asked James Greene, the Minister responsible, for his views but he denied issuing any such orders. However, *The Guardian* has received a copy of the memo issued by Greene to all hospital trusts in England and Wales and it says: '*No treatment may be given to anyone without first checking their name, address, NI number and cross-referencing against their passport or photo ID. In the case of foreigners of any nationality, no treatment may be given before a suitable means of payment is furnished by the patient and payment is taken in full. There are to be no exceptions to these rules.*' It is signed James Greene, Minister for Immigration.

The next day, *The Guardian* featured a similar article from the Manchester Primary Health Trust, concerning the death of another Indian visitor. That afternoon, the *Daily Telegraph* ran a feature on two Indians in a North Yorkshire hospital who were about to die without treatment; one Nigerian woman who had fled from her home in Northern Nigeria after being gang-raped by a bunch of Muslim extremists, only to be told that no hospital in England or Wales could treat her unless she could pay £5000. She committed suicide two hours later. The *Telegraph* finished by asking the public and all hospital trusts to notify it of any other incidents. There were more than twelve thousand responses.

Day after day, *The Guardian* and *Telegraph* ran articles detailing thousands of cases in which hospital treatment was denied to sick people, even those coming from the European Union. One case involved an elderly Frenchman who suffered from angina and, having left his heart tablets behind him at his home in the North Loire valley, asked a hospital for an emergency supply. He was apparently told that they could not supply him because they did not believe he was a European Union citizen. He protested his right to the medication and it seems that the effort was too much for him, because he suffered a massive heart attack. Even so, it would appear that the hospital left him on a trolley until he died without treatment. The authorities said that he was unable to furnish them with a means to pay for his treatment. It was pointed out to them that the patient was unconscious and therefore incapable of paying. The hospital responded by saying that it was under strict orders from the Minister for Immigration in this matter.

James Greene picked up the phone to his Cabinet colleague David Baillie the Health Secretary, and said, "David, have you seen the daily papers?"

"Indeed, I have James."

"What are we going to do about it?"

"Not my problem, James. It's all yours," replied David.

"But we're in this together. It's a joint venture!" exclaimed James.

"Not so old fruit," was the reply. "It's backfired and your name is on all of the memos and directives, not mine. You chaired all of the meetings and the whole committee will back me up. I've already spoken to the Prime Minister on this issue and said that I was against it from the start. I only went along with it because I thought it had Prime Ministerial backing. I've also got a statement from Mary Williams, you know, the woman you sacked from the Care Quality Commission at the first meeting, and she says in no uncertain terms that she was against your ideas. In fact she goes further to say that most other members of the Committee told her that they were also against your ideas but were too scared to speak up in case they were sacked too. So you see, my friend, you've got one almighty problem and I'm having nothing to do with it." There was a pause and David said, "Oh, I believe the Chief Whip wants to see you tomorrow at 9 a.m. sharp. He muttered something about you requiring help to draft your letter of resignation. Well, I could be wrong James. Yodel-o," and with that he hung up.

The headlines in the next day's *Guardian* read: **'Home Secretary James Greene Resigns in Disgrace'.**

The phone rang. "Hello, Bill Fillingrue-Smythe?"

"Bill, John Prendergast. Hello. Yes. I just wanted to say well done. We've finally nobbled that little shit and I'll tell you something, it feels bloody good."

"I quite agree John. *This* is immigration and revenge; a sterling job thanks to you."

"Me? What did I do?"

"Well, those James Greene memos to the Primary Care Trust executives that you doctored."

"Oh that. Well I only left out the bit about not denying life-saving treatment. Anyway, how are you enjoying the Knighthood?"

"Pretty good John. In fact it's damn good."

"Be seeing you at some of the better Whitehall and Livery functions no doubt. I've just got my CMG letter. This morning."

"What?" said Bill. "You're a Commander of the Order of St Michael and St George?"

John replied, "Not yet Bill; not until the autumn but it's in the bag once you get the letter. I gather I'm the hot favourite for Permanent Secretary once Sir Joseph gets the Cabinet Secretary's job."

"Well done!" said Bill. "Can't think of a more worthy recipient."

"Thank you, Bill. Most kind. Fancy a spot of nosh to celebrate? How about Axminsters again? OK, see you there, say 12.30. Let's make it an extended lunch. I'm sure there's plenty to discuss."

The front page of *The Guardian* read as follows: **'Two Leading Opus Dei Members of Parliament Found in Bed Together'.** It explained how Opus Dei numeraries swear a strict vow of celibacy, which can never be broken as they are symbolically brides and bridegrooms of Jesus Christ. It went on to explain how Liam Burns and Kate Jones were discovered in bed together in a hotel in High Holborn. The article continued: *'Apparently their affair had been going on for some weeks before The Guardian, acting on a tip from the public, discovered their sordid little affair.'* This was followed by lurid photographs, the most damaging of which was Kate Jones giving Liam Burns an intense blowjob. It continued: *'We asked the Auxiliary Bishop of Westminster, James Herrington, the Head of Opus Dei in the UK, for his views but he declined to comment on the subject. We requested the views of the Nuncio of all the Roman Catholics in the UK, Cardinal Basil Wharmsley, but he was unavailable. Finally, we asked the Prelate, the Head of Opus Dei, Cardinal Javier Echevarria, for his views but he denied the existence of the Order. So, ladies and gentlemen, I'll leave it to you to decide what's going on in this top secret Roman Catholic organisation.'*

Liam Burns was in his office in the Palace of Westminster when his phone rang and Liam answered it. It was his Monsignor.

"Can you meet me this afternoon, Liam? No, the lobby will do. I want you to meet someone. It's very important."

They agreed to meet half an hour later.

"Something important?" asked Bernard, his government colleague.

"I don't think so. It's just an old friend who wants to talk to me about something religious."

"Oh, I see. Not really my cup of tea, Liam. For a minute I thought you'd decided to sneak off for a small snifter, maybe more, with a lady friend." The look that he received made Bernard Chalk quickly exclaim, "Just a joke, Liam. It was just a joke, nothing more!"

Liam studied his colleague and said slowly, "It was not in the best of taste, Bernard."

"No. Well. No. Maybe not. I'd best go. See you after lunch or whatever. Sorry," and with that he left the office.

Monsignor Peter Morris was on time and he and Liam shook hands firmly.

"Liam, my son, how are you? I'm glad you could meet me. It's something very important. I want you to meet someone." He led Liam out of the Saint Stephen's public entrance and hailed a taxi. "Westminster Cathedral please driver," he said and they both sat back in silence. On arrival at the Gothic church off Victoria Street, they were met by Father Joe Evans, who led them to an office on the second floor. This, the office of the Auxiliary Bishop of Westminster, was as ornate as its occupant, Bishop James Herrington, who beckoned them both to comfortable armchairs in the corner. No refreshment was offered. The Bishop began, "Liam, remind me again how long have you been an MP?"

"Just over thirty years" was the reply.

"And how long have you been a senior member of this country's Cabinet or that of the Opposition?"

"A good twenty-five years I think."

The Bishop leaned forward slightly and said, "Yes, you've done well for yourself, that's for sure."

Puzzled and nervous Liam said quickly, "I hope I have done good for others and followed the teachings of God, your Excellency."

Gesturing towards Peter Morris, the Bishop said, "That was our view as well." He paused, looking carefully at Liam and then continued, "How long have you been a numerary of Opus Dei?"

Liam thought for a moment and replied, "I think for all of that time. I really wanted to become a Deacon of the Order and then be ordained but daily circumstances have repeatedly stopped me from being a useful servant to our Order. Don't get me wrong, I have endeavoured to help the Order in various ways over the years ..."

The Bishop went to a small table by the door, and, retrieving a newspaper, said, "Have you seen today's news, *The Guardian*?" He continued, "There's no need to turn over the pages; the front page, I think, says it all." He handed the paper to Liam, who took it with an innocent curiosity.

His face dropped and he developed a noticeable tremor as he looked at the photograph of Kate indulging in oral sex, quite clearly, with him, his lips curled back, enthralled in carnal pleasure. His arm dropped to his side and the newspaper slid from his grasp onto the floor.

The Bishop continued, "Can you explain this Liam?"

"No, I cannot," replied Liam.

"How long has it been going on, my son?"

"About a month, your Excellency," was the reply.

"I see," said the Bishop looking at a small tear in the carpet and pondering his next words. The silence was broken by Liam saying, "I suppose my nomination for membership of the Equestrian Order of St Gregory the Great will be revoked by our father Prelate?"

The Bishop sighed and said, "I should imagine it would, my son."

Liam was visibly crestfallen and had clearly resigned himself to his perceived fate, which he assumed he knew. He did not.

The Bishop said slowly, "I'm sorry Liam. I am the bearer of further bad tidings. You see, as a numerary of the Order of the

Opus Dei, you swore a solemn vow to remain celibate but you have clearly breached your vows. Regrettably I must tell you that our Mother the Holy Roman Catholic Church has revoked your membership of our noble Order, effective as of today."

Liam said quickly, "As a numerary surely, not as a member of the Order per se? I can still be an Associate and serve the Order. Associates don't need to be celibate, do they?"

"I'm sorry Liam. The Prelate has been so outraged by what you did and how you did it, so publicly and so sordidly, that he has personally expressed his opinion that he never wants to hear of you again. He says that, so grievous is your mortal sin that he feels only the Holy Father himself can give you penance and absolution. I am sorry, my son."

Liam could not believe what he was hearing; his whole life had come to an end.

The Bishop continued, "I must ask you to accompany Mgr Morris here back to Netherhall House and that you clear all of your belongings from your room by 6 p.m. today. You will, of course, leave your Cilice and whip for the use of others." Moving closer to Liam, he placed a hand on his right shoulder and, pushing him to his knees, offered his right hand with its Episcopal ring for Liam to kiss.

He then left the room accompanied by his attendant priest.

The silence could have been cut with a knife. Liam, however, knew what he had to do. First, he would go with his Monsignor to his hall of residence, hand in his property and then make his peace with his God who had forsaken him.

They found him two days later in his room, hanged by his belt with his bible opened at the page after his Saviour's crucifixion, the one where Judas hanged himself. Luckily, Liam's bowels had not opened up as he expired.

The meal in Axminsters ended excellently. Bill thanked John Prendergast, who picked up the tab, and putting on his long cashmere coat, Bill thought of his many achievements. He was *The Guardian's* most successful Editor-in-Chief; sales were soaring. He had got rid of the sanctimonious Liam Burns and ruined his chances of getting a papal knighthood. He'd well and truly rogered that shit James Greene's political career. Now no-one would touch him with a bargepole; he was regarded as high maintenance. He'd got himself a knighthood and even at this moment he was sure that his wife of forty years, the plump Lady Julia, was out buying dresses for the many formal events that they would be invited to.

Although he was not a religious man, Bill thanked God for His grace and vowed that if He wanted anything then He was just to give a sign. God obliged.

Bill stepped out into Jermyn Street, straight under the wheels of a speeding delivery van and was despatched straight to Heaven or Hell, according to God's will.

The front page of the next day's *Guardian* read: '*It is with regret that The Guardian has to report that Sir William Fillingrue-Smythe, the former Editor-in-Chief of this newspaper, was run down by a vehicle in Mayfair and was pronounced dead upon admittance to hospital. He will be sorely missed. His funeral will take place at St Boneface's Church in Berkhamstead this Thursday at 11 a.m. Lady Julia and her two sons have asked for privacy.*'

Immigration and Diplomacy

Sir Donald Evans, Her Britannic Majesty's Ambassador to the European Union, sat pensively in his first-class seat on British Airways flight BA176 to Zagreb, the capital of Serbia. He was a man of religious tastes, by which I mean he drank, smoked and expressed himself in moderation, as was the norm for most senior diplomats. He considered that he had a narrow path to tread between the conflicting interests of several parties of interest; those who favoured increased powers given to the European Commission in Brussels, which meant increased unification into a federal empire based on the Venetian model, against those who favoured the majority of power being vested in the nations comprising the European Union and therefore a more insular approach to European membership. However this was a situation of which he had much experience, namely the resolution of conflicting dichotomous agendas, which could be resolved either by getting all parties to compromise or by the exclusion of those perceived to have the least political influence. The only trouble with the latter approach was that today's tin-pot little African nation, ruled by an ignorant, pompous warlord, could turn into an influential Zimbabwe, still ruled by an ignorant, pompous President. Sir Donald had learned long ago that it was best not to insult political parties, especially where natural resources were involved and of significant interest to western countries.

The Serbian Government had asked the Foreign and Commonwealth Office to send a senior diplomat to meet its President and Foreign Minister and no reason was given for the visit. Sir Donald speculated that it had something to do with Serbia's desire to become a member state of the European Union, a quite understandable desire for the country's leading politicians to line their Swiss-based pockets with the generous financial grants and loans, which should have been destined to realignment infrastructure projects but were invariably diverted to the personal use of third world countries. Sir Donald understood the exigencies of these situations but did not see why he was needed in Zagreb. What did the Serbians want from the UK and what would they be offering in return?

At immigration, he went through the VIP channel and, flashing his white diplomat passport, was efficiently whisked through and a messenger was sent off to retrieve his luggage, which comprised two small crocodile skin suitcases. "Sir Donald?" asked a tall, slim man, who was immaculately dressed in a dark blue lightweight suit, white cotton shirt, black silk tie and a pair of highly polished leather moccasin shoes.

Sir Donald said, "Yes."

"I am Valery Zukov, First Secretary of my country's Foreign Ministry. Welcome to my country, Sir Donald. Did you have a pleasant journey?"

Sir Donald indicated that it had been uneventful and asked, "What is the agenda for my visit, Mr Zukov?"

"My Minister felt that you might like to go to your hotel first and then join him for lunch at 1 o'clock, if that is convenient for you."

Sir Donald looked at his watch; it said 9.30 a.m. He smiled and said, "Yes, that would be quite convenient."

Just then, his luggage arrived and Valery led them to a large, comfortable, black Mercedes, which moved off slowly into the morning's rush hour traffic, its red, blue and white pennant flapping on the front offside. They travelled downtown amid a bunch of concrete buildings, the same the world over, that signalled the city's financial centre.

"My Minister thought you would be most comfortable in the SAS Radisson Hotel. We hope you find it to your liking. Please say if not and I shall arrange an alternative."

"I'm sure it will be fine," said Sir Donald.

They arrived at the hotel within thirty minutes of leaving the airport and Sir Donald noted that it was the same faceless glass and white marble edifice as those in which he had stayed throughout the world. He was greeted warmly by the hotel's general manager, who arranged for Sir Donald's luggage to be taken to Room 1501, the presidential penthouse, dispensed with the formalities of check-in and accompanied Sir Donald and Valery to the room. Upon entering, Sir Donald was taken aback. The suite was large, with a bedroom complete with an oversized bed, a spacious lounge complete with a full-size well stocked bar but the thing that took his breath away was the incredible view over the rooftops of Zagreb, to the distant mountains to the north and the beautifully laid out national park to the east.

"I hope you find this room to your satisfaction, Sir Donald. If there is anything you need, please phone on extension one. My name is Jacovitch Vatchev," and with that he bowed slightly and left the room, closing the door behind him. Valery turned to the Ambassador and said, "Sir Donald, I have arranged for a Ministerial car to pick you up at 12.45 to take you to lunch with the Minister. I shall arrive with the car as you would expect." He bowed slightly and left the room. Sir Donald looked around, marvelling at the opulence of the hospitality shown to him. He thought, *they must want something urgently from me.* He glanced at his watch; it said 10.15. He quickly stripped, had a hot shower and changed into his fawn, lightweight Italian suit made from the finest cashmere, accompanied by a pale yellow crisp cotton shirt made by Tyrwhitt's in Jermyn Street. He rounded it off with a golden silk tie and a pair of highly polished brown brogues, which, although imparting great elegance to his dress, were far too heavy for a continental climate, in Sir Donald's opinion. He resolved to obtain a few pairs of elegant shoes from Milan next time he was there.

He went to his bar, not a mini bar but a full-size commercial bar. He found a miniature of vodka and diluted it with fresh tomato juice and finished it off with a twist of lime; he preferred the taste to lemon any day. He also preferred the use of vodka because it was so easily disguised on the breath. In any case he would take a quick rinse with CB12, a marvellous product he had just discovered. It kills the bacteria and sulphur compounds that cause bad breath and it offers protection for up to twelve hours. Just the thing for a busy diplomat, thought Sir Donald. Sometimes he'd felt a little guilty about his drinking habit but he concluded that it was a vice he could live with, especially because he was away from his wife for at least three weeks in every month, did not pick up call girls, nor go out on the town with his colleagues and, if he were to indulge somewhat more than was wise, he could always blame it on tiredness from travel or maybe a suffusion of excellent wine served to him at official functions. That usually got him out of any difficult situation. He also found that smiling and saying little also helped. He helped himself to another, rather larger cocktail, served this time in a large piebald glass, without ice. He felt nicely refreshed and walked to the balcony overlooking the city. For a country embroiled in war for many years, Serbia had certainly done well in Sir Donald's opinion. The phone rang and announced that Mr Zukov was downstairs with the Ministerial car. Sir Donald thanked the operator and said he would be right there.

The journey to the Foreign Ministry took just six minutes, as it was supposed to do. The chauffeur opened the rear door and Sir Donald stepped out to be greeted by another official who simply said, "Good morning sir," and deferred to Valery Zukov, who led the Ambassador up the Carrera marble steps and into the Serbian Foreign Ministry. They walked quite a long way along exquisitely carpeted corridors, on each side of which were ornately gilded doors. Eventually, at the very end of one of the longest corridors they stopped and Valery knocked on the door. "Come in," was the reply and there, in the centre of one of the most ornate rooms that Sir Donald had ever seen, stood the Serbian Foreign Minister, who walked towards the Ambassador with his right hand outstretched.

"Ambassador," he said, warmly shaking Sir Donald's hand. He continued, "How good to see you and so quickly. I shall try not to disappoint you in our important discussions. Come, please sit with me." He indicated two Louis XV chairs.

"Well, I must say that you live well, Mikhael. It's better even than the Foreign Office in London. Quite magnificent, in fact."

Mikhael Bogdev smiled and said casually, "Thank you, although I cannot take credit for any of it. These offices were, in fact, the summer palace of the last Czar before he was thrown out by the Communists. We've tried to treat them with respect ever since we ousted the party officials who took power in the late 1960s. They were real peasants, more at home on a tractor than in a palace. Do you know what one of them tried to do? He wanted to throw out all of this furniture and replace it with synthetic leather sofas and foam cushions. We managed to rescue all of the furniture and stored it in the basement until the corpulent incumbent died of a heart attack a year later; too much vodka was the reason. Anyway, forgive me, I am talking too much. Shall we have lunch?"

They walked together to a door at the left-hand corner of the reception room and entered an equally sumptuous dining room laid out with three settings. "I hope you don't mind but I've invited Valery to our talks," said The Foreign Minister. Sir Donald shrugged to indicate his agreement.

A waiter arrived and Mikhael asked, "Pre-lunch drinks, Sir Donald? We have a particularly fine selection of vodkas. Do you know them?"

"I particularly like them," said Sir Donald. "I'll take the blue label if you don't mind, straight but maybe with a little ice."

"Ah, I see you are a well travelled man." He turned to the waiter and said, "Two. Large – no larger than that. We have thirsty negotiations ahead of us. What will you have Valery? Just a mineral water. Yes I forgot, Valery does not drink on duty. Very sensible Valery, just leave the drinking to the older men." The drinks arrived, "To us!" They all toasted.

The food arrived. It was what you would call a Huntsman's meal: a selection of cold cuts of meat, with many different varieties of cheese and pickles and then, as the main course, hot roast suckling pig with wild mushrooms, turnips, sauerkraut and sautéed potatoes. The finest Serbian wines accompanied each course: deliciously creamy Chardonnays, rich oaky clarets and exquisitely rich and fruity sweet wines to accompany the fresh fruits of the forest desserts.

Most people do not understand that Serbia and, in fact, most of the Central European countries, produce exceptionally fine wines. Take Bulgaria, for instance. It has been producing the finest red and white wines for over two hundred years but the West has not heard about them because they were consumed internally or shipped to the Communist elite in the Kremlin in Moscow. The white wines come from grapes in the Rousseau region on the south bank of the Danube and the tastes range from the finest Rieslings to the heaviest oaked Chardonnays that one would sample in Burgundy or in the Casablanca Valley in Chile. The red wines are legendary and apart from featuring the classic blends of Cabernet Sauvignon, Merlot and Cabernet Franc in the traditional proportions of 60%, 35% and 5% respectively, they can out-compete any traditionally produced French claret. However, Bulgaria has a secret weapon when it comes to red wine. It is the grape variety called Mavrud, a rich ruby-coloured berry which makes a sumptuous heavy red wine, similar to a robust Burgundy. Vintage ports, brandies and sherries of all natures from finos to olorosas complete the full range of elegant beverages.

"So, Mikhael, what do you want?" asked Sir Donald wiping his mouth on the heavy cotton napkin, his eyes regarding the Foreign Minister steadily.

"We want the United Kingdom's help in securing Serbia's admission to the European Union. Your Government is particularly well regarded by other leading members, such as Germany, France, Spain and Portugal, so it is logical that I should come to you." He paused and then continued, "Can you do it, Sir Donald?"

The Ambassador looked down at the marquetry in the dining table and replied, "Possibly, but there would be conditions, of course."

"Of course," said Mikhael, "I expected little else. What do you want?"

"Well, there would be a lot of money involved if Serbia should be successful in its application. We would like it."

"What? You want Serbia to hand it all over to the UK. Is that what you are saying, Sir Donald?"

"No. No. No. Not at all! What I am saying is that my Government would want your government to bank in London, rather than Berlin, Brussels, Paris or Zagreb. You know that the City of London has a large number of, shall we say, creative financial products available in circumstances like this. Products that would entail the payment of a consultation fee to senior members of your Government, with the funds being transferred to a suitable tax haven."

"Like Switzerland, for example, Sir Donald?" beamed the Foreign Minister.

"No, not Switzerland, Minister. We are expecting to negotiate a closure of that tax loophole within the month. You see, the European Commission has wanted to get its nose into that trough for several years now and the Swiss banks, being as pragmatic as they have always been, have agreed to levy a withholding fee against all foreign bank accounts without disclosing the identities of the account holders. The withholding fees will be transferred to the Commission in Brussels and should be substantial. So, in the end, the Commission gets its hands on more money, which it can squander on incompetence and corruption throughout the European Union and the Swiss banks can demonstrate independence and anonymity for their wealthy clients." Sir Donald paused.

"So where do you suggest, Sir Donald?" asked Mikhael, a small amount of spittle appearing at the corner of his lascivious mouth.

"Do you like holidays in the Caribbean, Mikhael?" he asked and receiving an enthusiastic nod of agreement, he continued, "Then I think you would be well accommodated by an account in, say, Grand Cayman or the Turks and Caicos islands. These accounts would be faced by bankers and lawyers who would preserve the anonymity of their trustees, namely you. They are unbreakable as my Government knows to its cost. No, I think those are your best bets, Minister."

"Thank you for your advice, your Excellency. I shall bear this in mind, Sir Donald." He paused, seeming to be undecided about his next question. However, he shrugged and asked it. "So, those are the terms? Do we have a deal?"

Sir Donald sensed a deal was almost concluded so he went in for the kill. "Just a couple of things, Mikhael. My Government would look very favourably on your country's application if it could guarantee, in writing of course, the kind of infrastructure projects which would automatically be assigned to British companies. After all, your country would be awash with European money and might as well have the best that that money can buy. Don't you agree?"

Mikhael's smile broke like the sun from behind a cloud. He said, "I see no problem at all with these conditions and I will arrange for Valery here to draft the necessary documents, for a fee, of course."

Sir Donald replied, "Europe would be more than willing to pay it."

They rose and shaking hands, Valery rang saying that Sir Donald required the Ministerial car to take him back to his hotel. Mikhael escorted Sir Donald by the arm to the dining room door and, as he opened it, Sir Donald turned and said, "There is another, very small favour about which I would like to request your help. It is very, very small indeed but I think it would be regarded as a significant gesture of goodwill by all concerned."

"By all means," said the Foreign Minister. He continued, "Please tell me about it."

The next day, Sir Donald Evans flew back to London Heathrow on flight BA 177 in first class. He did not know that Andrej Rakic was also flying to London in economy class, accompanied by two Serbian plain-clothes police officers. They landed mid afternoon to a dismal overcast sky and Sir Donald was met by a Ministerial car from the Foreign and Commonwealth Office, to which he was smoothly and speedily delivered.

Andrej Rakic, the Butcher of Belgrade and erstwhile leader of The Panthers, could not believe his eyes for there, in Terminal Two arrivals, stood his best friend and second-in-command Jovan Bulat. "Hello Jovan. What are you doing here?" They embraced warmly and on walking through the terminal, talked about the old times of valour and their vision to create a Serbia free of Muslim slime.

"I'm here for a similar reason as you, Andrej," he said. "Times are changing in our country. It's not the same as it was and our Panthers are being hunted down and killed. It's better we are here, free from their barbarity. At least we will have a chance to get some money together and live the good life in our big houses with beautiful, ignorant women all provided by this stupid government. Here, we turn this way."

"But this is not the main door Jovan," said Andrej.

"No, we're going out the back door to avoid the photographers who have found out you are claiming asylum here in the UK. They are not happy about it. This is the best way, trust me." They walked quite a long way through security protected doors and out to the back of the terminal. They stopped and Andrej asked, "What's going on Jovan?" Then he saw the 9mm Browning in his colleague's hand.

"I said to you times are changing in our country. It's not the same as it was and our Panthers are being hunted down and killed. You are the price of our country's entry into the European Union. I'm sorry Andrej," and with that he fired two bullets into the head of his one-time friend. Andrej was dead before he hit the ground. "I shall return on the next flight to Zagreb," he said to the two Serbian police officers. He continued, "I shall travel first class this time as befits a hero of our country."

Kenny MacDonald read the news of Rakic's death in his daily intelligence briefing papers from the Enforcement and Compliance Directorate and he thanked God for His intervention in this matter. Little did he know of Sir Donald's intervention and could not recall the Ambassador's question several weeks back in their meeting; the question was:

"I would be interested to hear what you would suggest we do with Rakic."

Question of Taste

"It's all a question of taste, you know," said Sir Joseph Malthouse, Knight Grand Cross of the Order of the Bath, biting a small piece from his garibaldi biscuit, his eyes studying my face to see whether he had convinced me. He decided that he had, or at least gone as far as he could for the time being. He stood up, offered his hand and said to call him anytime.

Yes, he'll do, Sir Joseph thought as he watched me close the door to his Whitehall office.

"Is that the new boy?" asked a tall thin man, about forty-something years of age, as he entered through a panelled door to the left.

"Yes, that's him," said Sir Joseph.

"Meeting go well?" enquired John, taking the comfortable green leather armchair underneath the Rembrandt to the left of Sir Joseph's desk.

"Yes, tolerably well; certainly worth having, I think," he answered. "I have a warm feeling about this one. I think he's a pragmatist, one who sees the larger picture and the needs of the nation as a whole."

"Well, I hope so," said John, putting down his cup and saucer on the highly polished surface of his superior's desk.

"If you don't mind, John," said Sir Joseph looking over his half-moon spectacles.

"What? Oh yes, sorry and all that," said John, removing the offending article.

Sir Joseph studied his deputy and mused how things had changed in the civil service during his time. He could remember quite vividly his first day in Whitehall and the start of his distinguished career, a career hard fought for and richly deserved. Well, some would say so and Sir Joseph and his friends were those who said so. But then he had always known what he wanted to do. Maybe that clarity of mind was the product of his strict Christian upbringing – his parents were Plymouth Brethren – or the expression of the beauty of his native Gloucester – ordered, dignified and delicate – like so many classical treasures.

He had always known that he would go to Balliol, get a double first, marry Isabel whom he had known since childhood and have two well behaved and intelligent children. All this had been achieved and was a great source of satisfaction to him. It represented a tradition, a personal history and that meant knowing who and what you are no matter what you are called upon to do.

Sir Joseph had often thought that the absence of tradition was the cause of many of the world's problems. It was all very well to have this fashionable tolerance of every crackpot faction of society, demanding the attention of the media (so easily given in the absence of real news), and the scarce resources of society. A lack of tradition manifesting itself in a personal vacuity, which those people tried to fill somehow, more often than not with a demand for approbation in respect of some obnoxious and extreme display of bodily interaction.

Standards had certainly dropped, he thought as he glanced at his junior; Deputy Secretaries were much different in his day. It was not that John lacked intelligence – he had a double first from Balliol, as one would expect. It was not as if he were unaware of the requirements of a situation; he had proven himself very capable in that direction during the necessary removal of the previous Junior Minister. It was perhaps that he lacked a certain style, a certain sophistication, a certain breeding, which manifested itself in the appreciation and practice of good taste. Yes, that's what was lacking.

"Yes indeed," said Sir Joseph aloud. "It really just boils down to good taste in the end."

And with that the Permanent Under Secretary to Her Britannic Majesty's Secretary of State for Home Affairs closed his diary and left for lunch at his club with his friend, the Head of the Home Civil Service and Secretary to the Cabinet.